To~~m~~ oops- Larry,

Enjoy o

SPILL

Dave

SPILL

Oil and Orcas in the Salish Sea

DAVE ANDERSON

ISBN-10: 1530433568
ISBN-13: 9781530433568
Library of Congress Control Number: 2016903881
CreateSpace Independent Publishing Platform
North Charleston, South Carolina

DEDICATION

To all those who have dedicated their energy toward protecting the orcas and the pristine environment of the Salish Sea.

ACKNOWLEDGEMENTS

As with most books, the author is just one of many people who contribute directly or indirectly to the finished product. This novel's genesis began when I learned of the proposed six fold increase in tanker traffic in Haro Straits should the trans-mountain pipeline's tripling in size be approved. Because of my legislative experience on environmental committees and as the legislative appointee to the Oil Spill Prevention Task Force, this set off alarm bells. I also had heard horror stories from my Prince William Sound fishermen friends, Roger and Don Bergquist, who had lived through the Exxon Valdez spill and it's still lingering effects all these decades later.

I naively thought I'd just whip out a story that would alert people to the increased dangers. Karen, my wife and partner in all my crazy ventures, deciphered my mostly illegible cursive and got it onto the computer so even I could read what I'd written. Ron Green, a high school classmate and career teacher, read my first very crude draft and made valuable suggestions without being so truthful as to discourage me. Early reads by Susan Berta and Howard Garrett of Orca Network and Ken Balcomb of The Center for Whale Research were valuable stepping stones. After advice from others that I take some writing courses, I eventually got into a writers group. Candace, Dan, Joanne, Regina, Greta and Chris spent innumerable hours making detailed suggestions for improvements and edits. Finally I began to recognize some of my own too long sentences, wordiness, and excessive adverbs and adjectives. My editor, Audrey Mackaman, helped propel me forward with character development, description, flow of the story and general editing. Elizabeth Person created the fine cover, maps and sketches. Longtime friend and recent author herself, Gloria Koll's final read and edits closed out this long process. Thanks to them all for the book's sake and for the orcas and our precious, fragile Salish Sea.

SERENDIPITY'S ROUTE • • • • •
TANKER ROUTES ||||||||||||

HARO STRAIT

WALDRON I.

STUART I.
TURN PT.

ORCAS I.

SPIEDEN I.

PEARL I.

SIDNEY I.

HENRY I.

ROCHE HARBOR

SHAW I.

SAN JUAN ISLAND

ANDREWS BAY

FRIDAY HARBOR

LIMEKILN STATE PARK

UNITED STATES

CANADA

VANCOUVER ISLAND

TANKER ROUTE FROM VANCOUVER

VICTORIA

PROLOGUE

Five short, low, reverberating blasts pierced the fogbank just ahead. From the cabin, Howard Strander heard his twelve-year-old daughter's frantic shout. "Dad! A ship!"

Howard leaped the two steps from inside the cabin to the cockpit and leaned over the other side to get a better look ahead from the thirty-two-foot rental sloop. His hands gripped the rail as he peered forward. The fogbank was impenetrable. It muffled all sound and wrapped all vision within its cottony haze.

"Dad!" Megan screamed again.

And then he saw it. The nine-hundred-foot container ship bearing down on them like some Leviathan. He felt a catch in his throat. His mind blanked.

It had been bright and sunny when they'd left Prevost Harbor just minutes ago to begin their search for Meagan's orcas in earnest. Seemingly from out of nowhere, as they rounded Turn Point, one of the San Juan's not infrequent August fogbanks loomed. Just as suddenly ahead, another ominous shape appeared. Off their vessel's port bow, Turn Point Lighthouse, once a beacon of protection for boats of commerce before modern electronics, stood watching, a silent witness to possible disaster. Would the previously welcoming San Juan Islands now turn on the Strander family?

Howard then heard on his outside VHF speaker the captain shout, without the customary introductory identifications, "You, sailboat there opposite Turn Point, don't you know what five blasts mean?"

This time it was Howard's fifteen-year-old son, Jason, shouting, "Look out, Dad!"

That snapped him into action. He didn't have much time. The now identifiable containership, with *Bel Amica* plastered on its sides in large letters, was longer than three city blocks, and hardly that length separated them from their collision course. Howard took his post at the wheel, revving the sailboat's forty-horse-power Perkins diesel. He spun the steering wheel hand over hand, hoping to escape toward the west away from the course of the oncoming monster. The boat came about under his command, turning away from Turn Point and the oncoming freighter out into the stretch of open water.

"Howard!" Karen had come up from the cabin into the cockpit. Looking to the south, she stood speechless with one hand clasped over her mouth. Howard looked up to see what had frightened her so much.

The *Bel Amica* had turned west, too.

"What am I supposed to do?" Howard snapped. He wished he'd paid more attention to the rental office's instructions about fog. But how could he know it would come from seemingly nowhere so quickly? And it was too late now. They were on a collision course.

They were so close they could hear muffled shouts from the *Bel Amica*'s bridge. The ship's horn blasted five times again, as if it would do any good. Then, surprisingly, Howard began to realize the ship was moving north toward Stuart Island. In response to the *Serendipity*'s attempt to escape to the west, the *Bel Amica* had turned hard over starboard to compensate for the *Serendipity*'s westerly tack. The monstrous ship turned as fast as it ever had, propelled by its own speed and the strong eddy current pushing hard on its starboard stern. It was now heading away from the Stranders, but directly toward Turn Point.

Seconds later they heard the prolonged, loud, low crunch of metal scraping rock.

SPILL

Almost immediately the family could see and smell the black goo, like molasses, begin pouring out of the *Bel Amica*'s port side. It could only be one thing, Howard thought. Oil. Tarry, barely refined bunker oil.

As the Stranders watched in disbelief, the *Serendipity* drifted to the south. The fog was clearing but too late to do anyone any good. The heavy chemical stench of bunker fuel increasingly washed over them. Howard felt it catch in the back of his throat, bitter and foul.

He had hoped this vacation would help him escape anything to do with oil. It had followed him, ironically, even here.

Chapter 1

Bismarck, North Dakota
Two weeks earlier

"Damn it, Howard!" Jim Stern said. "We need that permit approved and we need it now! Yesterday, even."

Howard nodded. Occasionally it was better to feign agreement. It was his job to keep Strander Oil Services' clients happy. And the North Dakota shale oil business was a good business. Howard didn't like doing business with them, especially since Jim seemed to think "environment" was a four-letter word.

"The boss is anxious to keep the rigs working," Jim continued over the din of drill machinery. "Rigs are hard to find and lease. Everyone wants to get in on the bonanza. And these wells are coming in better than expected. The farther north we go on this trend line, the shallower and richer" —he might have added "and cheaper"—"they are. So we need you to get us an accelerated timeline on the next permit application."

"I can't just rubber stamp these things," Howard said, exasperated. "Conditions...one second... Meagan, honey, get down from there."

Meagan groaned and leaned back from her perch on the railing to the side of the steps leading up to the oil drill platform and said, "Dad, we need to go."

Howard realized these onsite visits couldn't be very exciting for a twelve-year-old. "We're almost done here, honey," he reassured. His youngest always got anxious at the prospect of being late for her afterschool science club meetings. "Hard hat," he reminded her, prompting her to pull the bright orange helmet back to its proper place on top of her head before turning back to Jim. "Conditions down under change. You know that. It's the aquifer. We're getting close to the water table. If we move any faster, without closer analysis, we risk letting fracking fluid leak into the aquifers serving both the town and reservation. I'm just not comfortable with that without more analysis."

"Screw 'comfortable'," Jim scoffed. "Find a way to get the job done. Things are too good here to stop now. There's a lot at stake, oil down there for the taking. Just get that report done or..."

Howard didn't like the way he trailed off like that, as if daring Howard to call his bluff. "Or what?"

"There are other firms doing permits and locating oil deposits with 3D seismic technology. You know how the industry is. Word will get around."

So there it was. As much as Howard wished he could say he didn't need Jim, the both of them knew better, evidenced by the long pause that passed between them. In the background, machines whirred and clanked, and Meagan was now rocking back and forth on her heels, the picture of impatience.

"I'll go back and look at the data," Howard said.

"You know what you have to do." Jim offered a plastic smile.

Howard knew he was dismissed when a rig worker came over, pulling off his oil-soaked gloves as he addressed Jim, and the two launched into conversation about some drilling procedure. As they walked away, leaving Howard standing on the drill catwalk, Jim turned back and pointed a knowing finger at him. Neither said a word. It wasn't necessary. Jim had made his point.

"Come on, Meagan," Howard said, hoping he didn't sound as defeated as he felt, "let's get you to science club."

As they got in the car, Meagan buckled her seatbelt and then stared at the dashboard before stating flatly, "He wasn't very nice to you, Dad."

It always surprised Howard how observant his daughter was.

"He's under a lot of pressure," he said. "That's just the way men talk sometimes."

He reached into the glove compartment, pulled out the prescription bottle, one-handedly popped it open, and lifted it to his mouth, downing one OxyContin, then another. He chased them with the cold dregs of his morning coffee.

Meagan watched him. She knew what was in the bottle. "Do you have a headache, Dad?"

"No, honey. It's my back."

She nodded with the tacit understanding that her dad didn't want anyone questioning his way of dealing with stress.

After dropping Meagan off, the song "Take This Job and Shove It" played on the radio. Howard turned it up.

Karen was in the kitchen preparing dinner when he got home. Howard guessed his wife had gotten off early from her job at the reservation. The smell of sautéed onions filled the air, and she looked so intent upon her cooking, with her sandy blonde hair pulled back with a headband, her brows furrowed in concentration, that he couldn't help but come up behind her and wrap his arms around her playfully.

She gasped in surprise and whirled around to smack him with her spatula. He chuckled at her reaction. For a moment, Jim Stern was completely forgotten.

"Don't scare me like that." There was no real anger in her voice.

He bent over to give her a peck on the cheek, and she gave him a quick, playful pretend swat. "How was your day?" he asked. Then, catching another whiff from the kitchen stove, "Mmm, smells good…what's for dinner?"

"Meatloaf," she answered, setting the hot pad aside and turning down the heat on the stove. She turned from her work and began washing up in the sink. "Day was good. We got a lot done at the res'. How about you?"

"Hmm…" He stretched his arms over his head, working out the kinks in his joints. "Good, good. The project's going well. Everything's great." He plopped himself into the overstuffed armchair on the other side of the breakfast bar.

Karen washed her hands and came to join him, taking an adjacent seat on the couch. "How's the report coming on the next section?" She pulled her knees up and rested her hands on the couch's arm.

"Okay, I guess," he answered.

"What's the 'guess' about?"

"Just some little stuff. I'll get through it."

"What is it?" Karen persisted. She leaned her head on one of her hands and leveled her blue-eyed gaze at him. "I'm curious."

"Nothing big. The formations, you know. With this fracking, occasionally things get messy. You can't be sure just how much penetration you're going to get."

"But don't you want to break up as much formation as you can to get the most oil possible?"

"It's not quite that simple," Howard explained. "In this case, there's an aquifer—the one serving the town and res' wells—close to the target area. Drinking water could...well...worst case scenario, get contaminated."

Karen thought about that for a moment. As the reservation's environmental consultant, she could imagine the consequences of a contaminated water source. "Can't you just move your drill target farther away?"

"Not in this case," he sighed. "The best part of the formation is close to the aquifer. It's a large piece, with multiple wells going in, and it looks really rich on the 3D seismic."

"So what are you going to do?"

"I've got to finish the report somehow," Howard said. "Jim is really getting on me to finish it."

"So you're in charge of writing the report that would let it go ahead? And you're going to do it?"

"I don't really want to talk about it anymore." He stood abruptly, ignoring the way the blood rushed from his head. "When's dinner?"

———

Dinner at the Stranders' was a family affair, even if Jason spent most of the time texting his friends under the table.

"How'd practice go?" Karen tried to engage her fifteen-year-old son in conversation, but Jason was at the age Howard dubbed "monosyllabic responses only."

"Mmm," he replied.

"Think you're making enough improvements to have a good shot at making the golf team?" Howard tried. He knew his son was passionate about making the high school golf team, but trying to get the kid to say more than two words at a time was like pulling teeth.

"Mmm, I guess," Jason answered.

Meagan, on the other hand, couldn't stop talking, even as she shoveled forkfuls of food into her mouth. "We watched a movie today in science club," she began. "It's an old movie, but it was really good. *Free Willy.*"

"I remember that one," Howard said, leaning forward on the dining room table. "It's about a killer whale, right?"

"Right," Meagan answered, her cheeks like a chipmunk's with all the food she had packed in there. She swallowed, wiped her mouth with her sleeve—ignoring Karen's look of disapproval—and continued with her account. "It's about this boy who makes friends with a whale in an aquarium and decides to set him free. Because the whale misses his family and his fin's all droopy."

"He misses his family?" Howard asked in mock surprise.

"Yeah, Dad. Killer whales are really family-oriented. They're a matriarchy, and the boys stay with their moms their entire lives. They've done studies that show different pods have completely separate languages that only they can understand, and even whales that have been in captivity for years still recognize their pod's calls." She paused long enough to shove another mouthful of meatloaf in. "I'd like to see a killer whale in real life."

"Well, we've got a vacation coming up," Howard said, even as Karen shot him a look from the other end of the table, knowing of Howard's pressing work schedule. "Maybe we can make a trip to Sea World."

"No, Dad," Meagan said, looking him in the eye, which meant this was serious. "I want to see them where they live. You know, in the wild."

"Where would that be?"

"You know," Karen spoke up. She dabbed at her mouth with a napkin. "Aunt Patty says they have whales that go by their place on Puget Sound all the time. Don't you remember seeing orcas on our San Juan Islands honeymoon cruise?"

"Aunt Patty," Howard mused. "It's been years since we've been out to see her. Is she still near Seattle?"

"Anacortes," Karen corrected. "A couple hours north of Seattle. She's been begging us to come out there for years now."

"Can we go?" Meagan fairly bounced in her seat with anticipation.

"I don't know, sweetheart. Your father's work—"

As if on cue, Howard's cellphone rang. The stilted ringtone broke the rhythm of the table, and Howard reached apologetically into his pocket. He stood, pushing his chair back as he felt his stomach drop to his feet. "Sorry, I've got to take this." It took him several paces to reach the hallway, where he could speak in relative peace. "Hi, Jim. What's up?"

"I'm not catching you in the middle of anything, am I?"

"No, no, it's fine. What can I do for you?"

"Listen, Howard, I'm not sure we left things very clear earlier. So I'm telling you as your friend, we *need* to have that report soon. If you can't produce it, for whatever reason, the boss will find somebody who can. Do you understand?"

Howard took a deep breath to still his nerves. "I understand."

"Good. So, when can we expect it?"

"Oh, uh…" Howard glanced around the corner to where Karen, Meagan, and Jason were still at the table. "I've sort of promised my family a vacation."

"What, now?"

"Well, you know, school starts in a couple of weeks. I can take my laptop and finish the report as I vacation."

Jim paused, and Howard could hear him sucking on his teeth in deliberation. "Okay, if you have it absolutely finished and on my desk by Monday after next, I think we can make that work."

After Jim had hung up, Howard's back pain re-emerged. He went to the bathroom, located his hidden backup supply, and popped a couple more oxys before rejoining his family at the dinner table. "So, shall we go find Meagan's orcas?"

Chapter 2

Aunt Patty was there to greet them at Sea Tac Airport. Karen's sister looked a lot like her, with the same strawberry-blonde hair and heart-shaped face. A few years difference between them had deepened Patty's smile lines, especially evident as she waved them over and enveloped them, one by one, in enthusiastic hugs.

"Oh my, look how much you've grown, Jason!" She didn't seem the least bit put-off by the teenager's awkward A-frame hug. "And Meagan, you were little more than a baby last time I saw you. Why, now you're a young woman." Even though Meagan couldn't have remembered their last meeting, she still met Patty's hug with open arms. "I hear you're quite an orca enthusiast."

"Yeah, I wanna be a marine biologist when I grow up," Meagan replied after they'd parted. "I can't wait to see a killer whale, or hopefully a whole pod."

"Orcas, dear," Patty answered, tweaking Meagan's nose playfully. "They're not killers. The residents don't hardly eat anything besides salmon. And I don't think you'll have much trouble finding them this time of the year."

"You know a lot about ki—orcas, Aunt Patty?"

Patty smiled and nodded. "You learn about orcas when you take beach watcher training." She ushered the family to the car. "I'll tell you all about it on the ride to Anacortes."

Seattle was a beautiful city, situated on the clear blue waters of Puget Sound. The city, with its glass and concrete buildings, overshadowed by the Space Needle, soon gave way to pastures and forests guarding both sides of I-5 north.

Despite Washington State's reputation for gloomy weather, the sun was out as they turned off I-5 about an hour north of Seattle and followed Highway 20 west toward Puget Sound. They crossed the bridge to Fidalgo Island, where the portside town of Anacortes awaited them with its quaint maritime charm. Meagan's face was plastered to the window as they passed Victorian-era buildings, now restaurants, shops, and apartments, with murals of people painted along the sides—famous Anacortes residents, living and gone, with bright, cheerful smiles greeting returning visitors and newcomers alike. Even Jason glanced up from his phone to watch the scenery pass by.

The day was still early—that's what you got from flying west—and they reached the rental firm in plenty of time to pick up their rented sailboat. Karen had been the one to find the sailboat rental agency, after a phone call to Patty had informed them that they stood a better chance of seeing whales if they were on the water. In the end, they'd booked ten days on a thirty- two-foot sloop dubbed the *Serendipity*. It was a pleasantly appointed vessel. Howard listened with rapt attention as the representative went over the directions. "I understand from our earlier phone conversation that you two had sailing lessons while attending the U of W and that you honeymooned on a sailboat in the San Juans. But that was seventeen years ago, which puts you out of practice, so you've agreed to motor only," the agency representative reminded. "No sailing, unless, however, you'd like to spend a couple days in Anacortes to refresh on how to sail…"

"No, that's alright," Howard said, signing his name to the rental papers. "Motor only. Got it."

"I don't blame you," the rep said with an easy smile. "I'd want to get out on the water as quickly as I could. You folks chose a great time to come."

Howard nodded and glanced out to the west, where the San Juan Islands beckoned.

Howard knew from experience that motor sailing in the summer was easy. He remembered the waters were mostly protected from high winds and seas by the islands themselves. As they went over the operating procedure, the rep pointed out that navigation was now made significantly easier with full-color GPS showing the boat's relationship to the land and the sea bottom.

"Oh, just one thing, be absolutely sure not to get into any fog," she said as she finished showing them around the cabin. "You don't have radar to see the other boats or navigational obstacles in fog."

The cabin below was closed in but cozy and efficient with use of space, with a double berth in the bow. The dinette lowered down between the seats to make another smallish double berth. Meagan was excited by the prospect of "camping." Jason mumbled something about having to share a bunk and buried himself in the far corner of his booth-bed to play with his cellphone.

The cabin's woodwork was clearly done by a fine craftsman, using a soft, reddish brown mahogany. The entire cabin was tastefully decorated in an old-time sailing motif: nets, rope work, and old charts from Captain Vancouver's era. But as nice as the interior was, in Howard's mind it would pale in comparison to drawing up a chair on deck and watching the islands, back-dropped by the snowcapped Olympic and Cascade Mountains.

Just east of the marina, the sprawling complex of an oil refinery stood in stark contrast to the pristine Cascade backdrop. Numerous smokestacks spewed whitish exhaust while a huge black tanker docked for unloading, with another at anchor waiting to unload its crude oil. Patty, who had been pointing out sights and landmarks to them with such vivacity a few minutes before, grew solemn.

"There was an explosion at the refinery a few years ago," she said, her face grim. "Seven men were lost. One of them was a close friend's husband."

Karen cast her eyes downwards. "Sorry to hear that."

But Patty wasn't done. "A couple years before that, there was another petroleum-related disaster in Bellingham, up there by Mount Baker." She waved to the north, where the gently sloping shape of glaciated Mount Baker stood. "A gasoline pipeline ruptured into a creek up there, where some kids were playing. When the gasoline ignited..." She trailed off, one hand on her chest, like the loss was still as raw and fresh as if it had happened yesterday. "The gas company didn't even..." She stopped abruptly, her horrified gaze on Howard. "Oh, Howard, I'm sorry. I didn't mean—"

Howard lifted his hand to quiet her. "It's okay," he said with a sad smile. "Even in the gas and oil business we know our easy petroleum-centered lives can come at a pretty heavy price for some. There's risk at every stage of petroleum production, from exploration and drilling, to transportation and storage. We try to take appropriate precautions, but accidents happen." He shrugged, knowing the gesture in no way matched up with the hideous loss of life the industry sometimes experienced.

Karen came up behind Howard and put her hands on his shoulders. She didn't always agree with his business, but she was never hesitant to defend him. "Everyone uses oil," she said. "It's a fact of modern life. We all drive and fly and use plastics. We're using oil to power this craft, even though we could be harnessing the wind. I like to think of myself as an environmentalist, but even my carbon footprint is huge compared to most of Earth's inhabitants. I can't cast any stones."

Howard squeezed her hand, both a thank you and an apology. He wished he didn't have to put her in such a predicament, but as long as their family continued to live on the profits from his business, she would always have to compromise her ideals. They'd had many a conversation on just this topic, and it remained one of the few issues straining their marriage.

Meagan came out of the cabin and asked, "Dad, what are those huge boats doing there?"

Howard explained. "They're oil tankers carrying crude oil from Alaska's North Slope, completing the trip from the end of the pipeline at Valdez some fifteen hundred miles to the north in Prince William Sound. The Sound," he further explained, "was the site of the infamous Exxon Valdez disaster in March 1989. Meagan, some fifteen years before you were born, one of those big oil tankers hit a reef not far from where they had loaded their crude. At least eleven million gallons spilled out into the pristine waters of Prince William Sound. Hundreds of thousands of marine birds died, along with thousands of marine mammals, in spite of efforts to save them. Perhaps of most interest to you would be the fact that many orcas also succumbed and their population plummeted."

Meagan interrupted. "Have they recovered?"

"I don't know. You'll have to ask when we visit the whale museum at Friday Harbor tomorrow."

"Thanks, Dad. That's not easy to hear, but I suppose they've done things so that it couldn't happen again, especially here. Haven't they?"

"I think I've read they've done some things, but I'm not very well informed about that. You might have to do some research to find your answer. Perhaps you can Google something on my iPhone."

"Good idea. I'm going to do that right now."

Douglas firs and junipers lined the rocky shores, growing thicker and denser farther from the shoreline. The islands rose from the sea like the humps of great sea creatures and stretched farther than the eye could see. Aunt Patty, who had joined them on the trip as far as Friday Harbor, named them all, pointing to Guemes, Cypress, Decatur, and Blakely. She pointed to the north, explaining, "You can even see the mountains behind Vancouver if you squint your eyes and look hard enough." It was a clear day, and the Cascade Mountains were out in full force, sharp shapes against the blue sky, their snow creating an almost strait line across their peaks. They seemed too picturesque to be real.

"Any whales yet?" Meagan asked as she came bounding out of the cabin. Her youthful exuberance broke the atmosphere as she clung to the railing, brown curls whipping in the wind.

"Not yet," Patty chuckled. "You're not likely to see them this close to port."

Meagan turned to her aunt with a kicked-puppy pout.

"But you never know," Patty continued, hand over her mouth to hold back a genuine laugh. "You might get lucky."

Meagan smiled. "Where are they usually, then?"

"Oh, it depends. They come up Rosario Strait just ahead, sometimes, but you're most likely to see them around Limekiln State Park, on the west side of San Juan Island."

Meagan turned from the railing and called over her shoulder, "Hey, Dad, we're going to be on San Juan Island, right?"

"We're headed there," Howard said. "We're going to spend the night in Friday Harbor, and it's not that far from Limekiln Park. Here, I'll show you." He stood up, feeling old as his knees protested the sudden movement, and gestured for Meagan to follow him to the dinette table, where he had a promotional real estate map of the San Juans on which he'd used a magic marker to trace their anticipated route. "We're here right now." He pointed to their location. "And we're going to travel all the way to here by tonight." He pointed to Friday Harbor, on the eastern side of San Juan Island.

Meagan leaned over, hands grasping the end of the table as she studied the map with the same intensity she studied anything she found interesting. "Aren't all these names Spanish?"

"Yes," Howard explained. His daughter was more science-minded, but she didn't seem to mind a quick history lesson. She stood in rapt attention as Howard explained the 1792 voyage of the Spanish explorer, Francisco de Eliza, pointing out how Eliza had been seeking a Northwest Passage between the Atlantic and Pacific Oceans that would have dramatically shortened the route to the trade-rich orient. He further explained that although Eliza never found the Passage, he'd left his mark on the Islands and local geography, giving names such as the Strait of Jan de Fuca and Decatur, Orcas, and Lopez islands.

"It's kind of ironic," Howard explained. "Eliza couldn't find the Northwestern Passage because it didn't exist…but because of ice now melting north of Alaska and Canada, it might, for better or worse, soon come to exist, at least for part of the year."

Meagan's eyes grew wide. "In science club, we learned that melting ice caps are caused by climate change. The teacher said it's already endangering polar bears. Do you think it could hurt the whales too, Dad?"

"Well, climate change is…" Howard coughed awkwardly. Meagan knew what he did for a living, and he realized it would kill him to admit his business might preclude her wish of seeing whales in the wild. And while Karen might accept the necessities of certain evils, Meagan's world was still untainted by the compromises of adulthood. He concluded forlornly, "It's complicated."

As the *Serendipity* approached the ferry docks just west of Anacortes, a ferry blew a single long blast to notify the parade of pleasure vessels of its presence and right of way. It quickly moved to the west, much faster than the *Serendipity*'s seven-knot-maximum speed. Its wake gave their sailboat a gentle rocking, and Meagan waved to the passengers aboard.

Aunt Patty turned to all the family members in the sailboat cockpit and explained, "Before I decided to join you, I warned Howard that you might encounter some heavy traffic crossing Rosario Straits just ahead, with the recreational boats going east-west, mostly commercial traffic going north-south, and that with another refinery to the north at Cherry Point, that you may even encounter an oil tanker. If you look to the south a mile or so, you can see it just so happens we're going to see a tanker up close."

"That's so funny. Remember, Dad, I said I was going to Google tanker safety? Well, I just finished reading a news article that popped up. Check out this article in the *Seattle Times* dated November 16, 1989. It reads:

"'Studies have identified Rosario Strait as the most dangerous tanker route in the inland waters of Washington State. Yet because of the location of refineries, this is the state's busiest tanker thoroughfare, with more than five hundred oil-laden ships sailing through it every year.

"'If there is ever a major spill here, its toll could be worse than that in Prince William Sound. Rosario Strait is in the middle of the delicate San Juan Islands and just a swift current away from the largest population areas of Washington State and British Columbia. All around it is the region's richest concentration of sea birds, marine mammals, clams, oysters, and commercial fish farms.

"'Among the hazards, the ship must thread a needle between two submerged obstacles known as Peapod Rocks and Buckeye Shoals. The jagged reefs are a mile apart, a crack compared with the twelve-mile-wide waterway in which the Exxon Valdez went aground in Alaska's Prince William Sound.'"

"Let me see if I can find those features on our GPS," Howard said as he began to move to a larger scale on his GPS screen.

Meagan leaned in to peer at the monitor and excitedly observed, "There they are, Dad," as she pointed two fingers simultaneously at Peapod and Buckeye. "Like the article said, they look pretty close together."

"You're right," Howard answered, "and that isn't the only narrow spot up through there. The route those big tankers must go through looks like an S-curve from some kind of car race. Those pilots must be pretty good, especially considering the current they show on the screen as up to five knots, with swirling currents also indicated."

"Dad, see that smaller boat just behind the tanker? I think that's what the same article calls an escort tug. It's there to help if the tanker gets in trouble. Another article I found, from the same newspaper, written only a couple of years ago, says that in spite of new safety regulations like double hulls, escort tugs, and speed limits, this stretch of water is still one of the riskiest in the world because of its natural features."

"Boy, that's a lot of information for a twelve-year-old to find in such a short time. I'm really proud of you, Meagan. You're going to help make this trip really fun and informative if you keep that up."

"Thanks, Dad. I know I'm having fun."

The large black tanker continued to approach from the south on a course perpendicular to theirs. Aunt patty interjected, "Nowadays there's something like one hundred tankers that sail through here every year. That's down considerably from former years due to decreasing production on the north slope, but they're all carrying about fifty million gallons of crude oil."

"Is that a lot?" Meagan asked innocently. She had perched herself just in front of the cockpit to be able to listen to Aunt Patty and to watch for whales, just in case.

Patty and Howard nodded affirmatively together. "And they may be increasing in numbers again," Patty went on. "They say as many as three hundred or four hundred more tankers will travel through adjacent waters if a proposal for an enlarged pipeline from the Calgary area passes."

"Would they really allow something like that?" Karen asked. "It seems to me that would increase the risk of an oil spill substantially." She stopped to ponder what she'd just said. "You haven't had any big spills around here, have you?"

"No, not yet. But we've had some relatively small ones and some close calls." Patty shook her head. "A few years back, a pretty good-sized fuel barge sank right up there." She pointed ahead towards Rosario Strait. "Fortunately, it only lost about one fifth of its four hundred thousand gallons. Also, a few thousand gallons went overboard on another tanker as it was unloading in Anacortes, and the resulting oil slick stretched clear to Deception Pass." She pointed south, towards Deception Pass Bridge, which Howard knew from studying the maps was six or seven miles away. "There were also spills of a couple hundred thousand gallons in the Port Angeles Harbor and a couple of a similar size on the Washington coast." Pointing to the south down the Straits, Aunt Patty said, "See those low islands, called Bird Rocks, barely breaking the surface? Two women, who were concerned about the possibility of a major tanker spill from these tankers heading up through these waters, wrote a novel, *Superspill*, depicting a hard grounding and major spill, fifteen years before the Exxon Valdez spill in Prince William Sound. Hopefully that scenario will never be realized here."

The tanker up ahead, which had just passed by Bird Rocks, was heading due north. Its current trajectory looked to take it near the *Serendipity*'s path in a few minutes if they stayed on their present course. This would be their first inter-vessel navigational challenge. Howard dropped his speed to a crawl. He wasn't taking any chances this early in the voyage, and the tanker passed well in front of the *Serendipity*.

The tanker's wake shook the small sailboat. Karen ran to snatch Meagan back from the railing. They waited for the motion to subside. An escort tug followed behind the tanker, and the captain waved to the Strander family.

The waters calmed significantly after the tanker passed, and Patty went back to pointing out sights of interest and then pointed to the north. "There's where the Peapod Rocks and Buckeye Shoals you just found on your GPS screen are."

Howard tried not to think about the giant tanker that had just passed by.

Patty continued with her verbal tour. Perceiving discomfort from Howard, she didn't say anything more about the tanker. "James Island," she said, pointing south. "Entirely a marine state park with good anchorage and docks on both the north and south sides."

"Any whales there?" Meagan asked.

"Sometimes they come by this way, but not recently." She turned her finger to the next island, a small clump of land to the southwest. "That's Decatur Island. The folks living there prefer to avoid pesky summer tourists, so there's no public ferry. Right across the way is Blakely Island, and between them is Thatcher Pass, where we're headed."

Jason, who had been sitting in a small nook next to the cabin trying in vain to find a signal for his cellphone, nodded and made noncommittal noises at every new landmark, most times not even lifting his head. Howard shook his head, hoping his son wouldn't spend the entire vacation like that.

As lunch time approached, Karen broke out cooked Dungeness crabs Aunt Patty had brought. The family sat on the deck, cracking crab, tossing the shells overboard. Meagan was hesitant at first, not used to the work that went into getting the crab from its shell, but once Howard taught her how, she dug in with the same relish she had for most of Karen's home cooking.

As they exited Thatcher Pass into an open body of water, Aunt Patty pointed out two of the three largest San Juan Islands, with Lopez to port and Orcas to starboard. Later they passed the well-named Flat Point on their left, where two boats stood moored near one another, each with a man perched on a pole looking down into the water.

The family was entertained watching a little skit play out as a couple of fisherman scurried down from their observation tower perches and, with the help of two others, quickly pulled up a net with a couple dozen very lively fish. One fisherman grabbed a fish by the tail, faced the *Serendipity*, and signaled Howard to come alongside.

"Want a humpy?" he hollered.

"Is that a salmon?" Howard replied

"Sure is." He hefted the fish, a couple feet of wriggling scale and muscle. "It's yours if you want it."

"What would I do with it?" Howard spread his arms wide. "I'm not any good at cleaning fish and we don't have any ice."

"Tell you what," the fisherman retorted, "I'll clean and ice it for you."

"Oh, that's too much," Karen argued.

A mere minute later, as the smiling fisherman reach across to hand Howard the iced and bagged fish, Howard reached for his wallet and asked, "What do I owe you?"

The fisherman laughed. "It's on me. Reef netters don't get much for humpies, so they're more fun to give away than sell. If it was a sockeye, we'd have to charge you $20.00."

Howard grinned. "Well then, it will be my pleasure. I'll take it. Thank you very much."

"Why do they call them humpies?" Meagan asked.

"Because of the humps on their backs," the fisherman replied, pointing to the fish's back through the plastic bag. "It's more prominent on the males when they get close to spawning."

Meagan considered that for a moment before asking, "Do you ever catch Chinook salmon?"

"Not so many nowadays, young lady. There used to be more."

"What happened to them?"

"Who knows?" He shrugged. "I guess the killer whales ate them all."

"But weren't there actually even more killer…er, orcas around before when there were many more Chinook?"

"Good point. You got me there."

The *Serendipity* slowly motored away, the family waving as two of the fishermen climbed back up to their perches to watch into the clear blue-green water through polarized glasses for more approaching salmon.

Chapter 3

F riday Harbor, on the eastern shore of San Juan Island, was a bustling town in the summer. Its colorful shop-lined streets greeted visitors before they even set foot on land. The marina was crowded with boats as the Stranders pulled in and tied up. It was a veritable floating village in its own right with ships of all shapes and sizes. The boats transitioned from recreational to mostly commercial fishing boats farther up the dock. However, white fiberglass pleasure vessels overwhelmingly dominated the scene.

The family spent their first night aboard and set out in the morning, heading uphill following the street signs that directed them to the Friday Harbor Whale Museum. Jason grunted something about not wanting to go to a museum on vacation, and they left him at a coffee house where he hoped to get a signal on his cellphone. The rest of the family made their way to the museum. Meagan skipped along with excitement on light feet.

The museum itself was a small two-story building overlooking the harbor. It may have been small—Meagan was initially wary when she first caught sight of it, more used to displays like those at the Omaha Zoo—but it made use of its room by packing it full of displays. Skeletons of sea life, from seals to sea lions to orcas, hung from the ceiling or lounged in glass cases. Charts and posters littered the walls, while information videos played in darkened rooms. It seemed everywhere they went the sound of whale calls followed them.

A museum worker with a nametag that read "Mary" approached them, hands clasped in front of her and a gentle smile on her face. "You folks have any questions?"

"Are the whales really endangered?" Meagan pointed to a troubling graph that seemed to show a decrease in the whale population over the years. *I hope that's not why we haven't seen any,* she thought.

The docent replied. "Well, it's not looking too good. The total number of resident orcas has declined from one hundred down to eighty-four between 2000 and today."

"Why?" Meagan pressed.

"That's difficult to say. Probably a combination of factors. A scarcity of Chinook salmon, toxins, increased noise. The sound from large vessels, like freighters, tankers, even naval anti-sub sonar testing, has had a very detrimental effect on orcas and other marine mammals."

"Because they use echolocation, right?"

"Right." Mary seemed impressed. "Loud noises interfere with their ability to navigate, communicate, and hunt, and the sounds put out by naval sonars can reach levels that are physically painful and damaging, even lethal. Also, while toxin levels are a little lower in recent years due to less industry along our shorelines, there's been a steady increase in non-point pollution. That's anything that doesn't have one specific point of origin, like runoff from homes, lawns, boats..." She shrugged helplessly. "You name it."

Meagan contemplated these facts soberly. "We'll still get to see them, right?"

"You stand a good chance of seeing them," Mary said before adding, "even if your grandchildren might not." She reached into the apron of her uniform and pulled out a phone. She turned on the screen and turned it towards Meagan to give her a good look. "These pictures from Haro Strait were taken yesterday," she explained, pointing to the cluster of black dorsal fins breaking from the water's surface. "In fact, if you sign up at Orca Network's website for sighting alerts, you'll get location updates on your phone every time they've been spotted."

"I hope Jason found a signal for his phone," Meagan said. "It'll be the only thing he's good for on this trip."

Her mother gave her a disapproving scowl.

"Your family will almost certainly see orcas on the island's west side if you stay in the area for two to three days," Mary went on, pocketing her phone. "J Pod has been sighted around there recently."

"J Pod?" Meagan asked.

"The resident whales live in groups we call pods, designated with letters J, K, and L," Aunt Patty said, speaking up rather unexpectedly.

"That's right." Mary raised her eyebrows, recognizing a fellow orca follower. "J, K, and L Pods are our resident whales, meaning they live mostly near here. They eat fish, preferably king salmon, while transient orcas—the ones which occasionally pass through Puget Sound—typically eat only marine mammals such as seals, sea lions, and porpoises." The docent shifted into her memorized-tour-information voice. "Transients generally live closer to the ocean but occasionally come in toward the Sound. Residents and transients don't mix. In fact, when they're near each other, they display signs of tension and the residents typically chase off the transients."

"And we know which whales are in which pods," Patty said, picking up the thread. "Each orca has a unique fin and saddle patch." She patted the small of her own back, indicating the location of the whitish-gray area just behind the dorsal fin on an orca. "Those areas are quite visible when orcas porpoise and breach."

"We give each individual a name, pod letter, and number," Mary said. "If you find whales…" She stopped to correct herself. "*When* you find whales, you can take a look on our website to try to identify who's who."

"Do you have any advice on the best route?" her father asked.

The two of them went over the maps together, and Meagan heard names like "Prevost Harbor," "Haro Strait," and "Mosquito Pass," though she didn't care if they had to sail all the way up to the North Pole as long as they found her orcas.

"I just can't wait!" She could barely contain herself as the family left the museum, heading downhill towards the shops and cafés.

Their first order of business was to find Jason, though Meagan didn't think he particularly added anything to their experience. They found him in the coffee shop. Or, at least, they found a person who looked exactly like him, but there was no way this kid—smiling and clapping along to an ensemble of singing men—was the sullen boy they'd left behind.

The ensemble consisted of twelve men, all dressed in blue and white sailor's stripes, with an array of musical instruments between them: guitars, mandolin, fiddle and an accordion. Meagan had to admit their spirited performance of sea shanties made it difficult to sit still, and soon she found herself tapping her foot.

Aunt Patty leaned in close to her and whispered, "The Shifty Sailors. They're a local group. That man there—" She pointed to the accordion player. "—that's Vern Olsen, their leader." As the song reached its final chords, Patty gave Meagan a gentle push forward. "Go ask him to play their song about orcas."

Meagan approached Vern, an older man with a silver-gray goatee and sailor's cap pulled down over a set of aviator glasses. Shyly, she reached out and tugged at the hem of his shirtsleeve. He spun on her, and she worried she'd upset him. But he greeted her with a kindly grandfather smile, and she felt emboldened. "Do you know any songs about orcas?"

"We sure do, young lady," Vern said, giving her a knowing wink. He turned to the other singers and said, "Let's sing 'Lolita Come Home.'" Before the musicians began the first chords, Vern said to Meagan, "I wrote this one myself," before grabbing his accordion and belting out the chorus:

Come home, Lolita! Lolita, come home!
You can swim in Puget Sound. This place is still your home.
Your pod is here to greet you, to help you freely roam.
Come home, Lolita! Lolita, come home!

Forty-three years ago in a cove called Penn
Just off Whidbey Island, you were six years old then,
Abducted by Sea World owners, a group of devious men.
They didn't care about your feelings, and would surely do it again.

Vern waved to the crowd, inviting them to join in. "Anyone who knows the words can sing along!" The café patrons began clapping along, and some joined in with their voices.

Six whales were captured with you, science was their ploy.
Your brothers and sisters were shipped abroad from London to Hanoi.
The other six have all died, you're the one whale still alive.
For thirty-odd years you've performed tricks—breach, splash, dive.

Forty-three boring years. Isn't that long enough?
Come on, Miami! Get off your duff!
Wasting away in a leaky tank doesn't seem like much fun.
Come on home, Lolita, to your state of Washington.

The café erupted into applause, and Vern and the Sailors behind him took theatrical bows, some overdoing it with large sweeping gestures of their arms, which only made the patrons laugh and clap louder.

"Is Lolita a real whale?" Meagan asked.

"She sure is," Vern answered. "I lived on Whidbey where they netted her and six of her cousins, brothers, and sisters."

"But orcas are family animals," Meagan protested. "You can't take them away from their families."

Vern's face grew solemn with the weight of memories. "It was pretty heartbreaking to see those babies netted and hoisted onto trucks to take them to the aquariums that bought them. You could hear them squealing for their mothers the whole time, and the parents circled around the capture site all the while, just trying to get to them. To make matters worse, five other orcas died in the capture effort. We learned of that when orca carcasses began washing up on beaches near the capture site. Their bellies had been slit open and filled with rocks so they would sink and cover up the scandal. One was found with a heavy anchor attached to it. The only good thing to come out of this tragic incident was it eventually led to a ban on future captures in Washington state waters. "

Meagan's eye began to water.

"Lolita's the only one left from that capture," Vern added as he placed his arm around her shoulder and gave it a comforting squeeze. "We're working real hard to bring her home, though."

"I hope they set her free," Meagan said, absentmindedly wiping at her eyes. "Just like a real-life *Free Willy*."

"Yeah," Vern agreed. "Just like a real-life *Free Willy*." He turned, saying, "Wait here." He returned shortly. "Here. Take this CD. A gift from us." He waved his arm toward the whole group of smiling performers. "It's got the Lolita song on it."

Chapter 4

Friday Harbor High School
8:00 p.m.

Howard regretted sitting in the front row when the heckling began. "Sit down and shut up!" one man shouted.

"Yeah, why don't you go back to your stinking corporate boardroom?" added a small woman swathed in earth-tone scarves.

It had been too early for Howard to hit the bunk and fall asleep, and he wasn't in the mood to work on that promised report as the family returned to the boat. He decided to wander uptown and see if anything interesting was happening. Inquiring with the night watchman at the head of the dock, the elderly gentleman mentioned that some kind of a meeting was happening about shipping oil through local waters.

The watchman elaborated, "I hear a lot of folks are pretty riled up about it, and it's about to begin at the high school gym—but, with the way I expect this town meeting to go, I almost feel sorry for the speakers."

"Folks, folks," the officiator said, raising her hands to quiet the crowd's irate grumbling. "Our guests are here to hear your concerns about the Aperture Project."

"Hear nothing!" someone else yelled from the back row. "They're going to do it whether we like it or not. Isn't the real purpose of all of this to make it look like they care about what we think?"

The officiator raised her hand again. "We need to maintain order if we're going to get anything done tonight. Do you think we can do that?"

The dissenter seemed to grumble a reluctant agreement, and the crowd quieted down. Howard checked his watch. Ten minutes into an hour-long meeting, and the presenters hadn't even gotten a word in yet.

They had chosen the wrong attire for this event, the three of them dressed in expensive-looking suits, starched white shirts, and ties. They sat in a neat line behind the table on stage. The first one, a too-thin man with bewildered eyes, had his hands clasped in front of him. He looked like this was the last place he wanted to be, trying to assuage locals about the proposed pipeline that would bring oil from inland Alberta to Vancouver, British Columbia. Perhaps he knew, as Howard already did, that there was virtually nothing he could say to alleviate these people's concerns.

Nonetheless, when handed the microphone, he cleared his throat and began, "Ladies and gentlemen, you are lucky to see the development of such an unprecedented project in your region. Not only will the Aperture Pipeline be the first of its kind with stringent environmental standards, it will also bring markets previously foreign to the Pacific Northwest straight to your backdoor. Indeed, over 98% of the oil brought in through our pipeline will be bought and sold here, in America, at significantly reduced prices. Furthermore, we'll be creating jobs—long-term jobs—to employ thousands of engineering, construction, and maintenance workers.

"But we at Aperture understand that you are concerned about the environmental impact of this proposal, and I'm very glad to tell you that we'll largely be limiting our construction to already disturbed lands—"

Jeering from the crowd made him falter for a second.

"Already developed lands," he continued, trying to raise his voice to be heard above the general disagreement. "And where we *are* intruding on sensitive wilderness areas, we have plans in place to diminish the impact on farmers, wildlife, and national parks. We are working with locals—including First Nation peoples—to make this process quick, clean, and beneficial to everyone."

"Thank you, Mr. Mills," the officiator said. She took the podium and addressed the crowd. "Questions?"

Mr. Mills cleared his throat to get her attention. "I'm not taking questions at this time," he said, straightening his lapels and sitting back down.

Howard sat back in his seat. It hadn't gone unnoticed by the crowd that Mr. Mills hadn't bothered to specify what any of these safety precautions were supposed to be, and the auditorium became a buzz of discontent.

Mr. Mills handed the microphone off to his right, to a man with rimless glasses whom the officiator introduced as a representative of the Vancouver Terminal Project, the reason a good portion of the Island had shown up tonight. He explained how, where the pipeline left off, the terminal would take over, as oil tankers would be loaded with fossil fuels to be shipped through Boundry Pass, Haro Strait, and the Straits of Juan de Fuca to refineries.

This new speaker, at least, had more confidence than his predecessor, taking up the mic and launching into his, admittedly well-rehearsed, spiel.

"First, I'd like to thank you folks for coming out tonight," he said. "We absolutely want to hear your thoughts and concerns. It is the wish of Aperture to work closely with the residents of these islands to reach a deal we can all get on board with. Now, that being said, let's not blow this thing out of proportion. Are there risks involved? Definitely. But let's remember the benefits as well. A new Vancouver terminal will bring more ships through this passage. More ships means more jobs, and more jobs means more money flowing through nearby communities. Let's boost this sagging economy, right!"

He paused, like a rock star waiting for the audience to join in on the song. Instead he got the awkward silence of discontent.

"But we also know your main concern is the environment," he continued quickly. "And that's great, because that's Aperture's main concern as well. We work tirelessly to make our business eco-friendly, and so I'd like to take a moment now to hear your questions."

Dead silence followed.

Finally, a woman in an aisle seat raised her hand, and an attendant ran to supply her with a microphone. "I want to know what safety precautions, specifically, your company has in place to prevent oil spills. I know many people here—" She gestured to the crowd. "—remember the devastating Exxon-Valdez incident some years ago."

Howard did. He'd had a summer job fishing on a salmon seiner in Prince William Sound during his college years before the oil tanker hit the reef while transporting crude oil in those waters in 1989. More than eleven million gallons of oil had spilled into the ocean. The spill spread over six hundred miles. He'd witnessed, first hand, some of the deaths of the birds and marine mammals, that happened in spite of efforts to save them. "Clean up" attempts, time had shown to be a cruel joke.

Howard shuddered to think of what such a disaster would do here.

He leaned forward in his chair to hear what answer the representative had to give.

"That's a legitimate concern," Mr. Glasses said with a plastic grin. "And we recognize there are certain risks involved in the transport of crude oil, but there are risks involved in any venture. We've certainly updated our standards since 1989. We now have double hulls, as well as advanced GPS's to lower the risk of ships running aground. Not to mention two-pilot shifts, one-way traffic, and back-up mechanical systems…"

"Yes, but what will you do *if* there's a spill?" the woman asked.

The representative fiddled with his collar, as if his tie were too tight. "Rest assured that we have a clean-up protocol in place for just such an event."

A man in the front row stood up, and Howard recognized him from the pictures he'd seen in the whale museum. Descriptions listed him as the museum's founder of the facility as well as explanations of how he'd dedicated him life to studying, identifying, and protecting orcas and other whales.

He was a bit older than Howard and sported uncombed hair and a bushy gray beard. Decked out in a red windbreaker, he didn't exactly scream foremost expert of orcas and founder of the Whale Research Institute, but under that beach-bum exterior, Kirby Jackson was a man who was as stubborn as he was passionate and knowledgeable about whales.

"These ships are carrying diluted bituminous oil," he began, making a chopping motion with his hand as he spoke. "Conventional equipment won't be able to pick that up. It's like trying to gather glue, making it much more difficult to recover than typical crude. Some of it will sink, as happened in the river affected by the Kalamazoo River train spill. That spill took many times longer to mediate than expected. Bituminous in the deeper areas of the Sound would never be recovered, killing biota virtually forever. Sir, I respect that you might think you're prepared for such an event, but the truth is, you're not. Nobody is. I'm here on behalf of the wildlife you put in danger by sending your tankers through here. In Prince William Sound, roughly half the resident orcas succumbed to the effects of oil, and scientists there doubt that transient orcas will be able to survive as a subpopulation, twenty-odd years after the spill."

"Thank you for your thoughtful comments," Mr. Glasses said with a cordial nod, though Howard could tell the argument slid off of him as easily as water off the oil he was here to represent. "We at Aperture care deeply about the environment and—"

The room erupted into flat-out boo-hissing, and Mr. Glasses's smile faded away. Howard didn't miss the deliberate eye contact he made with the officiator, begging her to end his suffering. She was merciful and asked for the next speaker to take the mic. The last company representative to speak was a high-strung-looking woman who appeared to hardly be out of high school. She leaned over the table to speak into the microphone, and her voice was shrill. Howard couldn't remember her title.

"It is an undeniable fact…" She sounded like she was reading from a teleprompter, or worse, index cards in front of her. There was some evidence for this when she paused to look down at the papers sprawled on the table. "… oil is a vital part of our modern lifestyle and our everyday lives. W-we…" She stumbled a bit, took a deep breath, and resumed. "We've been sitting on s-so-called 'green' technology for several decades now, and the truth is that, while we've made significant strides, we're just not at a place to compensate for even a fraction of the energy we get from fossil fuels."

She turned her index card over. "With massive industry…industrialization in China, fossil fuels are needed now more than ever to maintain standards of living. Modern…conveniences are raising the living conditions of millions… sorry, b-billions of people who benefit from personal transportation, heating, and…" She flipped another index card but couldn't seem to find her next point. Instead she sat awkwardly shuffling through the notes in front of her, then slowly sank back into her seat with a look of mixed relief and defeat.

"Thank you, Ms. Barnes," the officiator said. "Now, we did invite the Gather Coal Terminal Project folks to send a representative, but they declined our offer. We received an official statement saying they couldn't see how their Cherry Point project could have any effect on the San Juan Islands." She paused. "We're now going to be opening the floor to general questions."

"No questions," the first businessman reminded her.

"Then why are you even here?" someone yelled.

That was the cue for chaos. Everyone started clamoring at once, lobbing accusations, hurling statistics and what-if scenarios, trying to be heard above everyone else. The officiator was on her feet and trying to maintain order, but Howard took the opportunity to show himself out. He'd had enough of the din, and it was obvious that nothing of substance was going to be accomplished. The locals were very protective of their home, while the oil company seemed too protective of their profits.

With the high school gymnasium's doors closed behind him, it was a peaceful night. The summer air was balmy, and overhead the stars shone like crystal-clear pinpricks, unencumbered by big city lighting. Beyond, in the harbor, the Sound was about as still as it had ever been, with gentle waves bobbing the boats. Howard inhaled a long delicious whiff of salt air. He had always loved the smell of low tide, dating from the times he'd stroll Puget Sound beaches while taking a study break at the U of W. It made him feel alive, like this was where his soul belonged. The family was asleep, oblivious to the seemingly never-ending legacy of *oil* following him even here.

Chapter 5

The Stranders left for Prevost Harbor midafternoon the next day, purposely getting a late start to take advantage of the strong northerly current, in a couple hours, towards Stuart Island. As they motored out of Friday Harbor, the flat, calm water glistened as the sun warmed the air. The staffer at the chartering agency had told Howard that if he stayed close to the shore, any opposing current would be considerably less. There still being the last of the ebb, they took the advice. This positioned them close enough to shore to clearly see the nicely landscaped and varied, mostly tasteful affluent homes. There was some serious money along the northeastern shoreline of Rocky Bay: large windows and decks, the houses designed to blend in with the natural settings. Howard surmised these were signs of a population appreciative and protective of their environs.

Travelling northwest past San Juan Island, they approached Spieden Island, also called Safari by some of the locals, because former owners years ago had imported a variety of African wildlife. Big game hunting no longer occurred there, and today it served as a wildlife sanctuary to its exotic species. Jason sat with his legs dangling over the side of the sailboat, phone momentarily forgotten as he searched in vain for "lions or tigers."

The family continued to head north, Howard at the wheel watching his Garmin GPS, which he was finding indispensable. He'd been going over the charts again, and while the more direct route around the northeast side of Johns Island looked easier, Howard, feeling increasingly confident about his navigation skills, opted to follow the narrow channel between Jones and Stuart. It looked a little tricky with the still low-ish tide. According to the Garmin, they'd have only a few feet under their keel in the narrowest and shallowest place. But with caution, he thought they could do it, and it looked to be worth the close-up views of the rumored quaint picturesque passage.

Howard approached the pass cautiously, but he was swept through quickly by the flood current, accentuated by the constricted geography. The whole family enjoyed the nearby view of a band of sheep and quaint farmhouse and outbuildings.

After the pass widened and grew deeper, Meagan suddenly spotted commotion in the waters ahead and shouted, "Look, I think those are Dall's." Shooting out of the water and crisscrossing just off their bow, porpoises leapt playfully ahead of them. They weren't orcas, but Meagan was still entranced enough to watch over the side of the railing until the porpoises grew bored with *Serendipity*'s slow pace and veered north.

At the entrance to Prevost Harbor Marine State Park, the anchorages and docks looked full, but just as the *Serendipity* approached the small dock, a sailboat their size was pulling away. The perfect spot, except that it was behind a large, ostentatious-looking vessel. Howard approached the spot cautiously, realizing docking a boat was not like parking a car. He had to take into consideration multiple factors: momentum, wind, current.

He came in bow-first. Jason took the bowline, already tied to the bow cleat, and stepped onto the dock to tie off. Now all Howard had to do was turn the rudder facing the dock and shift into reverse. That pulled the stern into the dock. It worked, and he felt pretty proud as he tossed the stern line to Jason. He'd only done it one other time, under the instruction of the chartering agency.

A fiftyish-looking fellow from the boat in front came back to assist them. "Here, let me help you with that, son." He took the stern line from Jason and tied it to the cleat. Jason scowled at being shown up, but the guy seemed friendly enough, dressed in shorts, deck shoes, a broad-brimmed straw hat, and sunglasses.

"Thanks," Howard said. "We're pretty rusty at this boating thing. It's been awhile."

The man clapped his hands on his large belly and let out a hearty chuckle. "Hell, I'm a novice myself. Just bought *Victoria* here about a month ago. Birthday present to myself."

"Well, she's very nice," Howard commented, eyeing the expensive-looking forty-foot Hatteras.

"Good for getting to know the right people." The man winked and thrust his hand out for a handshake. "Bill Conover," he introduced himself. He had a firm, businessman-like handshake. "So, what brings you here, friend? Business or pleasure?"

"Family vacation. We're visiting from North Dakota."

"North Dakota?" Bill laughed, as if that were the ends of the earth to him. "We do a little business out your way. Never been there though." He tilted his hat back with his thumb.

"What kind of business?" Howard asked.

"Aperture Industries," Bill said. "Oil. Shale oil."

"I've done some work for Aperture," Howard said, and when Bill looked surprised, Howard elaborated, "I own a firm in North Dakota that identifies drill sites and writes permit applications."

Bill's face broke into a broad grin, as if he'd found a kindred spirit. "It's a wonderful and growing industry with virtually unlimited potential... Lots of money to be made. Isn't it just great, especially in times like these, to be doing so well?"

Howard replied, without much thought, "Yeah, sure is. Things are going good. So, you're here on business, I take it?"

"Yep." Bill squared his shoulders in pride. "Business has been great. My company's enlarging our pipeline coming over here from the Calgary area and upgrading the terminal up in Vancouver... I'm working on the tanker transport side of it now. I bought the boat so I could take folks out to get to know them. You know how it works. Greasing the skids, they call it. Bit of a history lesson for you. That's actually a term that came out of the early logging in this area."

"Really?" Howard feigned interest.

"We've got to keep the ball rolling or you know what could happen. Those enviro-wackos could mess things up for us."

Howard remembered last night's crowd's attitude towards the proposed increase in tanker traffic. "Have they been giving you a lot of trouble?" he asked.

Bill rolled his eyes. "You know those nut jobs. Trying to scare people with the prospects of oil spills. Global warming. Environmental disasters. Believe whatever the big government EPA tells them." He scoffed.

"Some of those enviros are pretty out of touch with reality," Howard said flatly.

Bill shook his head in agreement. "Anyway, I'd better get going. Business to attend to." He nodded cordially to Howard, then to Karen and Meagan, who had appeared on deck.

"Thanks for your help," Howard said, and Jason just rolled his eyes. Thankfully, Bill had already turned and headed back to his boat, completely oblivious to the teenager's bruised ego.

As the Hatteras puttered out of the harbor, Jason undid the cleat tie and redid it. He might not have been as quick about it as Bill, but he did it with the same measured concentration he used on his golf strokes. Over and under, over again, looping the thick rope around the dock cleat several times before the final half hitch.

He had just finished when another boat came in and occupied the newly vacant spot in front of theirs. Jason dropped the loose end of the rope and stood abruptly; Howard turned to see what could make his son's jaw go so slack. It certainly wasn't the boat itself, as it was decidedly humble compared to the recently departed one. Rather, it had to be the young lady at the wheel. Her long blonde hair was loose and fell to her waist, and she wore a pair of short cut-off jeans that Howard thought to himself he would never allow Meagan to wear when she got older. He judged her to be about Jason's age and...

Sometimes Howard had to remind himself that Jason was no longer the little boy he'd taught to play golf all those years ago. He was a young man, with a young man's interests, judging by the goofy grin that had taken hold of his face in that instance.

The object of his interest spun the wheel over and made masterful work of docking, as if she'd been doing this her entire life. An older man, perhaps fifty-ish, hopped off the bow to help tie up and waved when he saw the Stranders watching.

"Greetings, dock neighbors!" he called out. He had salt-and-pepper hair and sun-worn skin. "Doug Anderson," he said, walking over and holding out his hand. His handshake was firm, and his sharp eyes met Howard's straight on.

"Howard Strander, and my wife, Karen." He nodded to her as she stepped off the swim step onto the dock, and then to Meagan, who followed closely behind. "My daughter, Meagan. And that's my son, Jason."

"Glad to meet all of you." Doug had a pleasant voice and a pleasant smile. "My wife's still below deck, and the young woman you saw navigating our craft is our daughter. Sidney," he called out to her. "Sid, come say hello."

Sidney jumped down from the boat and came up behind her father. She had his same smile, though hers was luminescent with youth. Somehow, her eyes immediately found Jason, and she turned that thousand-watt smile on him. Poor boy didn't stand a chance.

"You jet ski?" she asked.

Jason nodded, though Howard was pretty sure he'd never seen a jet ski up close, let alone ridden one.

"I've got one. Want to hop a ride?"

Jason looked to his father.

"Sidney's an accomplished jet skier, aren't you, Sid?" Doug said, hands in the pockets of his faded Hawaiian shorts.

Sidney nodded, and with that charm, how could Howard refuse? "Go ahead," he said. "Just be back in time for dinner."

Jason smiled, actually smiled, gratefully, and when Sidney turned with a flip of her golden hair, he followed with a spring in his step.

Doug and Howard shared a light chuckle between them.

"So, what brings you here?" Doug asked.

"Just vacationing," Karen replied. She accepted when Doug offered another handshake, and Howard enjoyed the way Doug's eyes widened just slightly at the force with which his wife returned the gesture. "We're visiting from North Dakota, family vacation."

"We want to see orcas," Meagan said, breaking through the adults to wedge herself into the conversation. For a twelve-year-old, she was truly fearless.

"Ah, orcas," Doug said, drawing the word out. "We actually saw some the other day when we were in Rosario Strait, not too far from here."

"Gosh," Meagan exclaimed, "I'll bet that was amazing."

"Sure was. They were feeding, and you could actually see them flinging salmon into the air." He demonstrated, tossing an invisible fish over his head and pretending to catch it again.

"Dad!" Meagan tugged on his shirt like a little girl begging her father for an ice cream cone. "We *have* to see them. We just have to."

"We come this way every summer," Doug said. "If you're lucky you'll see whales around Turn Point, up near the lighthouse." He checked his watch. "A little late to get there tonight—it's about a half hour from here, but you won't see any whales in the dark. How about you folks join us for dinner? I grill a mean steak."

Howard looked to Karen, but her eyes were already alight at the prospect of not having to cook. "Well," he said to settle the matter, "how could I turn down an invite like that?"

The dinner turned out to be a dock affair, with the Andersons pulling the deck chairs from their boat and lining them up. Doug cooked steak and prawns aboard the *Marianne's* transom-mounted charcoal grill. Tanya, Doug's wife, served them on paper plates. Meagan happily ate a hamburger Doug had managed to rustle up, but there was no trace of Jason and Sidney. The five of them sat looking for them expectantly toward the harbor's northwesterly entrance, where the sun would be setting in an hour.

Tanya dabbed at her mouth with a napkin. She was a petite woman who seemed to be deliberate in every move she made. "Did you say your family is from North Dakota?" she asked, folding the napkin in half and setting it on her empty plate.

"Yes," Karen answered. "We've been there for, let's see, seven years now, I guess. More or less since the oil boom started there." She patted Howard's knee while balancing her plate on her lap. "Howard is a consultant there, writing drill permit applications and helping confirm the presence of oil prior to drilling. I'm an environmental specialist for the local tribe. We met in Seattle, at the University of Washington. I was studying chemistry and Howard geology. We met in a chemistry lab. I guess you could say our chemistry was good in a couple ways. We took a sailing class together to get our Phys Ed credits and honeymooned sailing in these San Juans."

Doug nodded and opened another bottle of beer. "Well, congratulations on being together for so long."

"How about yourselves?" Karen pressed forward. "What do you two do?"

"We live in Kirkland," Tanya said.

"Yeah, just east, across the lake from Seattle, if I recall correctly," Howard said in recognition.

"I'm a dental hygienist there. Doug works in energy. The two of us are working on our second marriages. Wouldn't you say, hon? Working?"

"I guess that's an appropriate term." Doug raised his beer in salute. "Here's to successful marriages."

"Here, here," Howard agreed. "And as to working on successful marriages, we're all 'working' or else we're probably in trouble these days." He took a long swig of his own beer. "So…is Sidney your only child or…?"

"Sidney is Doug's daughter, from his first marriage, but I love her like my own. I've got a daughter from my previous marriage too." Tanya stood and began collecting empty plates and cans in a plastic bag for recycling. She continued to speak as she worked. "We've found that blended families have special issues, you know, like who's the authority with whose kids and under what circumstances. But I think we're doing pretty well, don't you, dear?"

"That sounds like a loaded question." Doug did a mock double-take. "But all kidding aside, yes. A resounding yes."

"How old is your other daughter?" Howard asked, wondering why she hadn't been along.

"Oh, she's twenty," Tanya replied, and her mouth quirked downwards into a slight frown. "She couldn't be with us on this vacation because she's in rehab." She looked up soberly, catching Karen's gaze. Howard tried to decipher the look of sympathetic understanding that passed between the two mothers. "She's been battling a narcotics habit for a couple years. You can imagine the stress that creates with her in and out of treatment."

The conversation paused, and Howard worried that they'd spoiled the mood.

"Sorry to hear that," Karen said with such genuine softness in her voice that everyone seemed to relax a little. "That must be difficult on you. On the both of you. Did she...?" She seemed to consider her question, then reconsider it. "Did she get started in high school?"

Tanya tied off the plastic bag and set it down next to her chair. "During high school, definitely, but not because she was keeping bad company. I believe it started out with OxyContin for her soccer injury." She ran her fingers along one arm, tracing the pale blue veins up and down her wrist. "I'm guessing she used more than prescribed and got a little high. By the time we found out about it, she'd moved on to smoking heroin when her prescription ran out and oxy got too expensive to buy on the street."

Without lifting his head, Howard snuck a peek at Karen to look for any reaction. She had done the same toward him. Their eyes met ever so briefly, each pretending they hadn't looked toward the other. The bottle of OxyContin felt heavy in his pocket just then.

"She eventually ended up shooting up heroin." Tanya was still studying her veins, particularly those in the crook of her arm. "But she's getting better. She's making a real effort this time."

Howard contemplated his beer and was glad when Karen spoke up next.

"Sidney seems like a nice girl."

"She's a great girl. President of her class, plays on the soccer and water polo teams, practices her guitar nonstop..."

Tanya gave a dramatic roll of her eyes.

"We think she's on the right track. Her favorite thing is that jet ski, though. If push came to shove, I'd guess she'd pick that over everything else." He finished off his beer before adding, conversationally, "She's entered a few competitions and done quite well."

"Sounds like an impressive resume," Howard said. "It seems like Jason's taken notice."

"He seems like a nice young man himself," Tanya said. "A bit quiet though."

"Oh…" Karen waved her hand dismissively. "He's just at that age. You might not know it from just meeting him, but he's actually a pretty sharp kid. He's not terribly athletic—he prefers more cerebral activities—but he has a real passion for golf. One of those calculating, hand-eye coordination things."

"Yeah, hand-eye coordination with his stupid phone," Meagan spoke up.

Karen reprimanded her daughter with a sharp look.

"What about you, Meagan?" Tanya asked, leaning forward. "What are you into?"

"I like science a lot," she said. "I'm taking a natural science class this summer, and I think I want to be a marine biologist when I grow up."

Tanya raised her eyebrows in surprise.

"That's great," Doug said. "Know what you want, kid. Go for it."

Meagan beamed.

"Well…" Tanya clapped her hands on her knees resolutely. "I think it's about time for dessert."

Meagan's eyes grew wide. "What is it?"

"I've got a pie from Whidbey Pies." Tanya licked her lips in anticipation.

"Sure!"

Meagan and Tanya stood and headed for the *Marianne*. After a few seconds, Karen also stood and hefted the garbage bag over her shoulder. "I'll just take this in and see if they need any help." And then she, too, was gone.

Howard and Doug sat in amiable silence for a moment or two.

"So…" Howard began after the pause had begun to get awkward. "Did Tanya say you're in the energy business too?"

Doug reclined in his seat and stretched out his legs, which were pale where his khaki shorts didn't cover them. "A little different end than you," he said. "My firm—I use 'firm' somewhat loosely. It's basically just me. I have a gas-fired power plant in California. Very small, but I'm looking to expand. I'm working on a project to build a co-gen plant."

"Oh yeah?" Howard asked, genuinely interested. "What kind?"

"Greenhouse."

"Greenhouse?" Howard repeated, hoping to coax more information.

"As I'm sure you know, power plants produce a lot of waste heat." Doug pulled himself forward, hands held out to demonstrate his words. As he spoke, Howard saw a spark in those eyes, the spark of real passion. "I noticed a large tomato-growing greenhouse not too far from my plant and approached the company to see if they were interested in building some greenhouses next to my plant. Their answer was no, but they asked if I was interested in building a power plant next to their already existing greenhouses to supply carbon dioxide for growth and heat for the winter."

"Think you'll go through with it?"

Doug considered for a moment then nodded slowly. "Yeah, I think I will." He had a faraway look in his eyes now, that passionate spark still glimmering. He seemed to snap back to himself, however, and gestured towards Howard. "So, what about you? You're in the energy business too, I hear. Oil, right? Why don't you tell me about that?"

"Oh, well…"

"I've heard quite a lot about the oil boom in North Dakota. That must keep you pretty busy these days."

"Yes," Howard laughed. It was an uncomfortable laugh, but he hoped Doug wouldn't notice. "I've got plenty to do. Everybody wants to get in on it right now—or better yet, yesterday. Although with crude prices slumping things may begin to slow a little. Strander Oil Services helps find the good drill sites, mainly with 3D seismic technology, and then we write up the drill permit applications."

Doug let that sink in with a slow nod. "In the shale oils in that part of the country, you pretty much have to frack to get the oil moving, don't you?"

"Yes." It felt like an uncomfortable admission, though, to himself, it shouldn't have been. "Virtually one hundred percent of the wells get some frack."

"Have you had any problems? On TV I've seen some reports about methane in drinking water and so forth. Is that exaggerated?"

"We haven't seen that in our area, but disposing of the fracking fluids is probably our biggest issue. Most of our operators are careful with how they handle it, but there's always a small chance of contaminating an aquifer if they're careless."

"While we're on the subject of energy resources," Doug asked, "is that open pit coal mining in your area?"

"No, thank goodness, that's over to the southwest of us in Montana and Wyoming. But talk about pollution, I think that's a pretty nasty business. Funny you should mention coal. I happened in on a local town meeting in Friday Harbor on our way out here and they mentioned an effort to build a big coal port just up the coast from Anacortes."

Doug replied, "Yes, we already have coal trains going through Seattle and several smaller towns. I've read quite a lot in our local press about how they spew toxic ash and disrupt traffic."

"From what I know, I'd advise the locals to oppose it. I imagine the coal would be shipped to China. The last thing the environment needs is more coal-fired power plants. Their acid rain and pollution end up right back on the west coast."

"Thankfully there is considerable opposition already. I've read the Native Americans from Wyoming all the way to Cherry Point, near the Lummi Reservation, resolutely oppose it."

He was cut off from further discussion by the arrival of Sidney and Jason, both of them dripping wet as they walked along the dock. "Sorry we're late," Sidney said, wringing out her hair. "The waves were just too good to pass up."

"You have fun, Jason?" Howard asked.

He expected a single-word answer, but to his surprise, Jason burst into motion, waving his arms about as he spoke. "Yeah! Sidney really knows how to run it. Like, she can jump waves, really big waves. It was so cool."

"Looks like you fell in," Howard observed.

Jason blinked before realizing he was still dripping all over the dock. "We got a lot of spray," he said sheepishly.

"Sorry about that, Mr. Strander," Sidney laughed as she swung herself over the railing of the Andersons' boat. She rummaged around for a few seconds before returning with a beach towel, which she tossed down to Jason. "I'm not totally used to having extra weight on the back. It takes a little getting used to. The extra weight puts out more spray on the landing." She looked to Jason. "Seriously, those tankers put out the biggest waves I've ever jumped."

"You're supposed to keep away from bigger boats," Doug scolded.

Sidney looked a bit ashamed. "It's okay, Dad. We stayed well behind them and we were really careful."

"Yeah," Jason said, speaking up. "We were totally safe, Mr. Anderson."

"Well, well, well," a feminine voice said, and everyone turned to see Tanya reappear from the depths of the *Marianne*, a pair of pie-laden plates in her hands. "Looks like you two got back just in time for dessert. Thought you said you'd be back for dinner."

They glanced at each other but said nothing. Jason's eyes went straight to the ice cream slowly mixing with the purple-blue berries, and Howard swore he saw the boy lick his lips.

"Not so fast, young man," he said. "You haven't had dinner?"

Jason lowered his head and muttered something that sounded like, "Haven't."

"Aww, let the boy have his pie," Doug chuckled. "We're on vacation. We should enjoy ourselves a little, don't you think?"

In the end, Jason and Sidney joined them for dessert, Sidney sitting cross-legged and Jason dangling his legs over the edge of the dock. The pie was divine, and everyone hurried to eat before the ice cream melted.

When he was done, Howard leaned back and patted his stomach. "I think this whole meal was made in heaven."

"Amen, brother," Doug said. "No argument here."

Chapter 6

"Mornin,' Howard." Doug waved from his boat. At seven o'clock, the light morning fog had dissipated, leaving the marina bright and sunny. It was already warm and promised perfect weather. "Say, we're going to catch the ebb tide down Mosquito Pass past Roche Harbor. Should be orcas down that way. You're welcome to follow, if you want."

Howard raised his hand apologetically. "Thanks, Doug, but isn't that pass pretty tricky to navigate? I don't think I've got enough experience to—"

Doug cut him off. "That's fine. Better safe than sorry, eh? Well...maybe you'd like to meet up later?"

Howard thought about it, then nodded. "Sure. We owe you a dinner, after all. Maybe we can rendezvous in one of those anchorages on the west side of San Juan Island after, hopefully, seeing orcas. Our latest info from Orca Network shows them to be pretty consistently in that area the last few days. So with any luck we should be celebrating tomorrow night. Do you have a cellphone number or...?"

Doug burst into hearty laughter. "Pretty sure our kids have already exchanged numbers, Howard. Speaking of...there's Jason!"

Howard did a double-take as Jason emerged from the cabin, fully dressed and as presentable as he'd been on the trip. This had to be the first time he'd been up this early on a non-school day in his life. Howard didn't need to rack his brain to guess what the incentive was, but even less so when Jason said, "Morning, Mr. Anderson. Is Sidney up yet?"

"Well, look at this," Howard laughed, clapping his son on the shoulder. "What's the plan for today?"

"You must really be looking forward to getting out and seeing the orcas."

"Yeah, that'd be cool," he replied as he gazed expectantly into the cabin window of Doug's Bayliner. But seeing no life, Jason shuffled back into his cabin.

Doug knowingly raised his eyebrows and cracked a little smile. Howard rolled his eyes in acknowledgment.

Soon Tanya poked her head out the cabin door.

"Good morning!"

"Yeah, isn't it beautiful out?" Howard said. "Everyone always talks about the rainy Northwest weather, but we've had nothing but clear skies."

"It actually doesn't rain that much here in the summer," Doug said. "In Seattle, maybe a little, but we're in the rain shadow up here." He scratched thoughtfully at his chin as he cast his eye out to open water. "The weather *is* notorious for changing on a dime, though," he said somewhat ominously. "You folks take care of yourselves, okay?"

<hr />

After a quick breakfast, which Meagan and Jason wolfed down as if they hadn't eaten in weeks, Howard began to chart the day's journey. He wanted to take advantage of the ebb tide. Thanks to Jason's phone and the Orca Network website Meagan had him download, Howard found that orcas had been reported just east of Eagle Point heading northwest.

" Perfect!" Howard shouted, " If the orcas stay on their present course up Haro Strait, they should be somewhere near Limekiln State Park on the west side of San Juan Island about the time we're there."

Jason wandered out onto the dock after breakfast. No luck again this time, as Sidney was nowhere to be seen. "Hey, bud," Howard called over the railing. "Can you untie our line from the dock cleat?" Jason sighed, as if this were some unimaginable chore, but eventually bent to perform his assigned task.

A slight breeze slowly pushed the *Serendipity* away from the dock, so Howard didn't even have to demonstrate his growing piloting skills. He motioned for Jason to hop aboard, and just as the teenager had jumped up to grasp the railing, Sidney appeared on the dock, blonde hair in disarray.

"Jason!" she called out as they drifted farther apart. "I hope…I'm sure I'll see you again."

Howard feared Jason might mutiny and jump overboard to get back to the dock, but Jason had apparently resigned himself to the day's plan. He waved goodbye from his position at the railing as the dock area grew smaller and smaller behind them.

Thirty miles to the southwest, a much larger vessel was preparing to leave Port Angeles. The Panamanian-registered container ship *Bel Amica* en route to Vancouver had just filled her two-hundred-thousand-gallon fuel tanks built into the bottom of her hull. The scarcely refined bunker fuel was separated from the sea by an inch of steel.

Captain Petrakis was far from his Greek home, but it consoled him that tonight he'd be dining in his favorite Greek restaurant in Vancouver. A relatively short haul across the Straits of Juan de Fuca, up through picturesque Haro Strait and Boundary Pass, and finally across the Strait of Georgia to Vancouver, approximately four hours in all.

As Captain Petrakis maneuvered his vessel away from the refueling ship, he needed to make a tight starboard turn to pass astern of another container ship awaiting fuel. He ordered the helmsman hard over starboard, half speed ahead. The vessel responded nicely, its bow swinging clear of the waiting vessel. Captain Petrakis ordered his fellow countryman Dominic Vasilides, "Bring her around three-quarter throttle, dead ahead, Domi."

A moment later, Dominic yelled, "It's the rudder. It's stuck again, Cap."

"Quarter throttle!" Petrakis ordered. "Those cheap bastards won't spend money to fix anything! Someday they'll be sorry."

"She'll come around okay now, Cap."

"I see. In a different situation, we'd have a big problem. I told them to fix the rudder, but they're too cheap. The rudder's old, not balanced, and the steering gear's all worn out. Let's hope we don't have to turn over too hard. Too much throttle and she'll jam."

The ebbing tide took the Stranders out of Prevost Harbor heading southwest away from the shoreline. It was clear sailing until they approached Turn Point, adorned with its picturesque lighthouse. It was as if a giant knife had sliced the passage in a clean line: bright and clear on one side, thick fog on the other. The *Serendipity* was up against a fogbank so thick, Howard realized he'd be unable to see anything if he ventured farther. The scenery was swallowed by a wall of dense gray. Stillness overtook the waters. Howard slowed the boat to a crawl, unsure of how to proceed. His agreement with the rental agency said he wouldn't operate in fog, but this had come out of nowhere.

Meagan sat at the bow and pouted. "Stupid fog," she groaned. "We'll never see the whales like this."

"Sorry, honey." Howard gave an apologetic shrug. "I can't wave my magic wand and make the fog go away."

Meagan didn't reply, and Howard was reminded that Jason wasn't the only one growing up. The little girl who believed her father really could do magic tricks was long gone, along with Santa and the Easter Bunny. It seemed too early for her to move into the sulking teenager phase.

Speaking of which, Jason had made himself scarce since they'd left Prevost Harbor. No doubt he was below deck, trying to get a signal on his cellphone. Too bad they were smack in the center of a dead zone.

"Why don't you keep watch?" he called. "I'm going to go see what your brother's up to."

"Probably trying to call his *girlfriend*." Meagan said that last word with such disgust, Howard gave a silent prayer of thanks that she hadn't yet discovered boys.

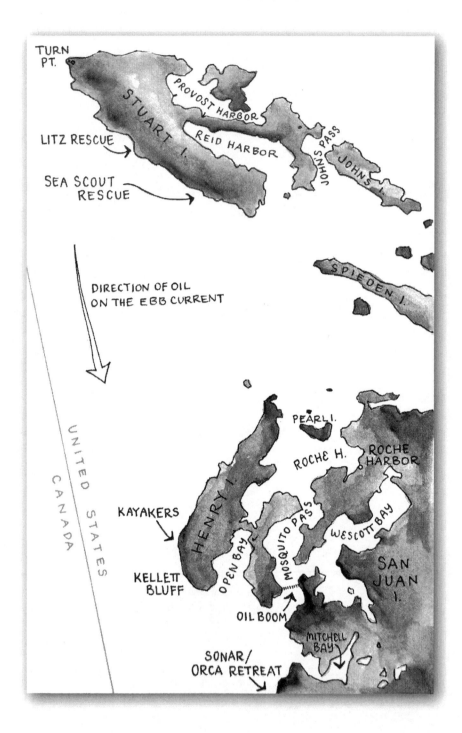

He found Jason doing more or less exactly as Meagan had predicted, albeit unsuccessfully. His thumbs ran across the phone's screen in rapid movements, and when that failed, he started smacking it against his palm.

"Hey now, careful with that," Howard reprimanded. "Unless you want to pay for a replacement."

"Stupid phone," Jason muttered, apparently oblivious to how similar he sounded to his little sister only moments before. "We need to get a better carrier, Dad."

"If you want to pay for it…" Howard repeated, holding his arms wide at the open-ended suggestion.

"Can't you just put in some overtime?"

Howard almost laughed at how comically his son had missed his point about financial responsibility that is until he remembered the OxyContin bottle in his pocket. He stopped dead in his tracks and ran a hand over his face. "Sorry, son. You know it doesn't work like that."

Jason glowered at him with that I-hate-you/I-wish-I-was-never-born/you-can't-tell-me-what-to-do look that Howard was sure he'd given his own parents back in the day. The fact that he'd eventually grown out of that phase didn't alleviate the pain he felt at being on the receiving end of it now. These kids! If work didn't put him into an early grave, teenagers certainly would.

He was about to say something reassuring and no doubt full of fatherly wisdom when five loud blasts jarred him back to the present. The noise seemed to rattle the very metal and fiberglass framework of their little sailboat, and hardly a split second later, he heard Meagan's scream.

"Dad! Look, a ship, coming from the fog!"

<hr />

George Petrakis cursed in Greek. "Damned sailboat!" the *Bel Amica*'s captain shouted, more to himself than to his first mate at the helm. "Don't they know that five whistles means get the hell out of my way?"

"We better do something, Cap, or there's going to be one less sailboat," responded the mate. Despite the levity in his voice, his hands remained loose on the wheel, uncertain. "What should I do?"

The little sailboat was directly in their path, and while David might defeat Goliath in storybooks and fairy tales, in the real world, the big guy would come out on top. Especially when that big guy was thirty times longer and thousands of times heftier than its opponent. They'd crush that thing, and everyone aboard. There was little time to make a decision.

"Port!" Captain Petrakis ordered.

Dominic obeyed and pulled hard to port. The enormous ship began to turn. Thirteen knots didn't feel like a tremendous speed—hardly fifteen miles an hour, by land measurement—but it was easily twice what that private sailboat could manage.

"Captain, they're turning the same direction," Dominic cried.

"Damn it," Petrakis swore. "Starboard. Starboard!"

The first mate manipulated the rudder into a hard starboard turn. The ship turned as fast as it ever had, propelled by its own speed and the strong eddy current pushing hard on its starboard stern. It continued turning, even as it headed directly toward Turn Point.

"She's going toward rocks. Hard over port!" Petrakis yelled. "Turn her, turn!"

"She won't come about!" the mate snapped. "The rudder...she's stuck again!"

There were not enough curse words in Greek, English, or any language Petrakis knew at that moment.

SPILL

Chapter 7

Captain Petrakis ran one hand through his graying hair as the other flipped through the emergency response manual. This incident might give him a few more gray hairs when all was said and done. So many contact numbers, hotlines, addresses, emails…contact information for the freighter's parent company….a law firm's answering machine in LA, he suspected set up that way just for incidences like this for liability purposes. He'd already put in a call to the Spill Response Team in Anacortes.

"Should have refused to go until they fixed the rudder," Captain Petrakis muttered to himself, not for the first time. "Should have insisted, even if it cost me my job."

According to the company's vessel manual, they would send somebody to assess the vessel and any potential damage to the environment, but more likely it was to protect their image and, of course, most importantly, the company's wallet.

The manual made note that the ship in question was legally obligated to notify several other agencies, and so here Petrakis was, thumbing through pages of phone numbers and contact information.

"Coast Guard," the woman answered over the phone. Jesus, they were letting women into the Coast Guard now?

"Need to report a grounding."

"I'm sorry, could you repeat that? Do you need assistance?"

Petrakis sighed. Either his accent was too heavy or this woman was a complete idiot. Perhaps a bit of both. "Grounding," he repeated, trying his hardest to enunciate. English didn't come easily to him, and sometimes people treated him like *he* was a complete idiot because of it.

"Grounding," the woman repeated. "A ship's gone aground?"

"Yes. I am on *Bel Amica*. We have hit rock. Cliff. Grounding. Oil spill."

"Oil?" She'd caught that part, at least, and her voice jumped a whole octave higher. "Oh...uh..." He could hear her flipping through her own manual. "Is anyone onboard hurt?"

"No."

"You don't require medical assistance?"

"No," he answered. *No, not from you, ever!*

"But you are leaking oil?"

"Yes."

"Okay. You're up against the rocks? Have you tried to move the ship at all?"

"We are hard grounded, stuck, with fuel tanks ruptured."

"Okay, maybe best you don't try to move, then. You'll just tear a bigger hole in your hull and maybe do more tank damage."

Petrakis sighed in frustration.

"What was the name of your ship, again?" the Coast Guard woman asked. "The *Belam...*?"

"*Bel...Amica*."

"What company are you with?"

"Am with ...ah...well I have telephone number."

"Do you...uh, have an SED form, per chance?" She seemed to reconsider the phrasing of the sentence. "Do you have a full list of any hazardous materials aboard your vessel?"

His English might not be up to snuff, but even Petrakis knew SED was a Shipper's Export Declaration form. You didn't get to be the captain of a successful trading vessel without learning these terms. *Ugh.*

"We have..." He snapped his fingers for his first mate to hand him the incomplete manifest. "Electronics. Batteries: lithium ion. Pyrotechnics: barium chloride, manganese..."

"Pyrotechnics?" the woman interrupted. "As in...fireworks?"

"Yes, fireworks. We just come from China."

"Ah," she said in understanding. "Flammable?"

"Very."

"Is your vessel on fire?"

"No."

"No open flames?"

"No." He was beginning to sound like a broken record. The woman on the other end of the phone sounded too young to even know what a record was, and here she was trying to talk him through a situation he already had under control.

"Okay," she said. "That other thing you mentioned...batteries?"

"Yes, new kind, lithyin something..." He struggled as he reached for the manifest to correct his pronunciation. "There is note here in manifest. Um... it say keep away from heat sources or mechanical damage. I think I remember reading about that new plane...aah... the Dreamliner having problems. Wasn't there even a fire and having to ground 'em? And laptops or something with those kind of batteries have even started fire and even explode?"

"Captain, are the containers with batteries in close proximity to the pyrotechnic containers?"

"Computer went down when fuel fume detection sensor shut down electrical supply. I don't have list of where containers are located. Oh, we just fill our fuel tank in Port Angeles...two hundred thousand gallons."

"You're sure there's no fire."

"I told you...no!" If there were ever a more useless person on this planet, Petrakis did not want to meet her.

"Orca Network, Shannon Besser here. How may I help you?"

The voice that answered was raspy, and not a little panicked. "I...I'm not calling to report orcas, but...I thought I should alert you." The man on the other end of the radio took a deep breath, and Shannon wanted to tell him to take several more, calm himself down. "There's a...a ship has gone aground. There's...there's a big oil patch...."

Shannon spoke as clearly as she could into the microphone to offset his panic. "You mean a ship is pumping some oil in its bilge water?"

"No, no, no," the frantic reply came back. "The ship *grounded*—a big freighter—and now there's a bunch of oil coming from it."

Shannon felt her breath catch in her throat, but she swallowed her rising panic. It was important to keep your head level when others were panicking. Her mother had always told her that. "Okay, sir," she answered. "What's your location?"

"We...we're just off of Stuart Island. Southeast...uh...I have the GPS coordinates right here."

"Okay, sir," she repeated. She picked up a stray pen from her desk and searched around for a suitable piece of scratch paper. "Could I get your name?"

"H...Howard. Howard Strander. I'm here with my family, and...oh God, I don't know how much oil, but...but easily thousands of gallons."

"Mr. Strander," Shannon said in her firm school-teacher voice, the one her mother had often used on her as a small child. "Right now I need to notify the Washington Department of Ecology and the spill response folks."

Howard took another deep, chest-wracking breath. "O...Okay. I just...I just thought I'd let you know. You know, in case there were any whales headed this way." A pause. "There aren't, are there?"

"We'll deal with that if it comes to it," she answered, though she would be lying if she said that hadn't been one of the first concerns to pop into her head. Shannon and her husband had first started Orca Network up here in the islands and had been running it together for over twenty years now. To say their passion for whales was a bit on the fanatic side would be understating the situation. "But I can notify you if a potential interface with the orcas comes up. In a situation like this, it never hurts to be in contact with eyes on the scene. Is this the channel you'll be standing by on, Mr. Strander?"

"Yes. We're—my family and I—we're on the *Serendipity*. We rented...out of Anacortes... I'm so sorry. The ship was trying to avoid hitting us and it... I really don't know what to say."

"Wait, wait," Shannon reassured him, allowing some of the sternness to seep out of her voice. "You probably shouldn't feel responsible, if that's what you're worried about. This was inevitable. We've feared this kind of accident for years. That's the honest truth. All these years we've contemplated, almost expected such an event, and now we'll get the dubious honor of seeing how efficient the containment strategy will prove. Let's just move forward, and you've been quite helpful. Just stand by for now, okay?"

Another intake of breath, this one labored and weary. It was strange what you could pick up from people when you weren't face to face with them. "Okay," Mr. Strander agreed at last, as he took a pill from bottle in his jacket pocket for the sudden flare up of his pain. "I'll be here."

Shannon adjusted her headset and switched channels to the one she knew her love was tuned to in his car. "Jack," she said.

The radio crackled and her husband came on. "What's up, Shan?" As always, he tended to speak directly and too-close into the mic, making him sound like he had a mouthful of marbles whenever they talked this way.

"I just got a disturbing report." She waited a beat. "Have you heard anything about a ship going aground near Turn Point?"

"What? No. When?"

"Just now. I don't know if anyone was hurt. It didn't sound like it. But, Jack…it was a freighter that's spilling bunker fuel into the Sound, thousands of gallons of it, as we speak."

Silence from the other end. "Let me check the tide tables." She heard the flapping of paper. "Turn Point, you said?"

She nodded before remembering he couldn't see her. "That's right."

"Let's see here…" The flapping sound slowed as Jack found the page he was looking for. "Oh." It came out as a low, wet breath. "Oh, that's not good. Tide's ebbing strong to the south for another two or three hours. It's been reported to the proper authorities, right? The spill?"

"I imagine the captain's already put in a report," Shannon answered. She'd love to see what *that* transcript looked like, what excuse the captain could think up for running aground. "And the man who reported it to me—I directed him to monitor the oil's southerly progress. That's a good start, right?"

"Good, but not good enough." His voice took on a higher tone that Shannon couldn't chalk up to static. "We've got reports of the orcas at False Bay heading toward Limekiln State Park."

Shannon's breath caught in her throat. That would take them directly into the thick of the spill.

"We should call Kirby," she said.

"Yeah," Jack agreed, releasing a long, defeated sigh. "Maybe he'll have an idea about what to do."

He'll have an idea, Shannon thought but she doubted anyone really *knew* what to do in this situation.

Keeping her husband on the radio, she reached across her table for the old rotary phone they kept there. Her fingers found her old friend's number easily enough, and she chewed at her lip as she waited for him to pick up.

"Kirby Jackson," he answered.

"Kirby, it's Shannon."

"Shannon," he repeated, as if he had been expecting her call. "So, I guess you've heard the news then."

"Is it as bad as it sounds?" she asked.

A pause. "We might be able to protect the orcas if we work fast."

"Very fast," she said. "Kirby, you've got J Pod heading your way as we speak."

Another pause. "I know we need to turn them away."

"They might slow down to feed, but—"

"Not good enough. We need to turn them around completely. If they come in contact with that oil..."

"I know, I know," Shannon said. She'd been in Prince William Sound during the Exxon-Valdez disaster, had seen firsthand what it had done to the wildlife, not least of which included the whales. She didn't need reminding of how bad it could get. "How do we do that?"

A longer silence this time.

"Someone is on the scene there already," Shannon said, hoping this was helpful information. "The people that gave us the initial report. It's a family on a sailboat, but I'm sure they'd be willing to help out if they can."

"Hmm," Kirby said. "Yes, I have an idea."

Shannon picked up a pen and wrote Kirby's plan across a bit of lined note-book paper, nodding occasionally. "It might work," she agreed, although get-ting it into action might be difficult. "I'll give them a heads up and relay a brief sketch of your plan."

"Keep me posted," Kirby said. "I'll call the whale-watching boats and have them report the J's positions and headings back to me, okay?"

"Sounds good." She hung up and turned back to the radio. She flipped the dial back to the channel number she'd kept on a Post-it note. "Mr. Strander?" She waited for his response.

"Yes?"

"This is Shannon Besser with Orca Net. We spoke earlier."

"Yes. Yes, of course."

"Mr. Strander," she repeated. "There is something you and your family can do, but you need to listen very, very closely..."

———ɷ———

Meagan watched the thick, tarry substance spread over the surface of the water, turning everything black in its wake. It was moving so fast. "How are they sup-posed to stop that?" she asked and couldn't keep the words from quivering as they left her mouth.

"Honey, honey." Karen pulled her into a tight hug, turning Meagan's eyes away from the scene. "Dad's notifying the right people right now. Remember what Aunt Patty said about SOSA, the San Juan Oil Spill Association people? They've been trained for this sort of thing. They've got these floating things they call booms stored at strategic locations around the San Juans. They'll set them up to contain the oil as best they can."

"As best they can?" Meagan repeated. It didn't sound so comforting.

"They're good people, and they're good at what they do," Karen said, run-ning a soothing hand through her daughter's hair.

"Is there anything we can do?"

"Oh, honey..."

"Everyone!" Her dad came running out of the cabin, where he'd been talking to the whale people on the radio. He doubled over and breathed heavily for a second or two before gaining the breath to speak. "Everyone, I need you to listen up." He clapped his hands together. "We've got some work to do to help save the whales."

Chapter 8

Howard watched through a pair of binoculars as an orange inflatable pontoon craft motored their way. As it approached, Howard observed that the man at the controls had a determined set to his chin as he ferried his load toward them.

"Those are the speakers?" Meagan asked as she looked through the identical pair of binoculars—from the *Serendipity*'s cabin, courtesy of the rental agency. She stood like a lieutenant at Howard's side. "They don't look very big. Are they really going to work?"

"Sure," Howard said with a confidence he didn't feel. The boxy, black devices stacked on top of each other in the back of the orange inflatable didn't look that sophisticated, but the woman from the whale watchers had told them Kirby's plans usually worked. "Remember what the lady from the whale museum said? The whales hate the Navy's sonar noise. If we put speakers in the right places, the familiar unpleasant sound will hopefully keep the whales back from the oil."

Meagan lowered her binoculars. "I came all the way from North Dakota to see whales, and now I have to help chase them away," she sighed, blowing at her bangs.

Howard laughed, and after a second, Meagan joined in.

The thirty-foot, hard-bottom inflatable eventually pulled up alongside them, and the motor sputtered before turning off. Howard reached across and held out his hand. "Howard Strander," he said.

"Kirby Jackson." An amiable smile emerged from under a thick, graying beard. "Wish we were meeting under better circumstances, but the fact that you folks are willing to help out means a lot."

Howard felt guilt pierce him like a knife.

"It's the least I can do," he mumbled.

Kirby clapped his hands and said, "Help me unload these bad boys, would you?"

Kirby had merely encased two large boom box car speakers in waterproof plastic sheathing. He'd added lead weights so they would sink. The speakers and electric wires were attached to a stainless-steel salmon-fishing downrigger wire and winch. He demonstrated how the speaker wire plugged into the boat's radio/CD player.

"You really think this will work?" Howard asked, keeping his voice down. Meagan was hovering not too far away.

"Honestly, I don't know," Kirby answered with a small shrug. "These aren't exactly Navy-grade. We'll get about one-tenth the decibels those monsters get, but the whales hate it so much, it might be enough to drive them off. Since your vessel doesn't have downriggers like mine, I attached a rope so you can lower and retrieve the unit the old fashioned way."

Howard nodded, grateful for Kirby's forthrightness.

Kirby ran over the rest of the operating procedure for the speakers—it was fairly straightforward, and Howard told himself that there was absolutely no way he could foul *this* up—before Kirby hopped back into his raft. "Watch football, Howard?"

Howard was struck dumb by the question but nodded numbly.

"Good." Kirby revved up his motor. "We'll be spacing these things about a football field apart. Think you can judge that spacing?"

Howard nodded, more sure this time.

"Okay. Watch for my signal. If I move, you move to keep the same distance." He waved and pushed off from the Stranders' vessel, staying in a straight line with them perpendicular to the shoreline. The craft's motor rose in pitch every time it crested a wave.

Howard picked up his binoculars again, his fingers twitching as he waited for the okay sign from Kirby. Meagan clung to the railing beside him. When

Kirby eventually slowed and stood up, waving both arms above his head, she leapt into action. She had the tape playing before Howard could get the speaker in the water. It made a shrill screeching sound that had everyone on deck covering their ears. Howard hefted the apparatus over the side of the boat and watched it drop a few feet into the depths before he tied the suspending rope to the stern cleat.

⚬

Shannon Besser felt helpless sitting at her desk, one hand clenched around the radio mic, the other knotted in a white-knuckled fist in her lap. She was helping, she knew—passing information along was possibly the most important task during a crisis—but it still felt so horrible to be in this little office, so far away from the action.

The radio crackled.

"Check it out," Kirby said, coming in on the VHF. "J Pod's coming in. They're already starting to spy hop. I guess you folks on the Serendipity already know that means the animals are lifting their heads out of the water to look around, spying on the surrounding area."

Shannon nearly stood and clapped. "They can hear the sonar, then."

"Yep," Kirby answered. "They're either looking around for where the sounds are coming from or they're just trying to get their sensitive ears out of the water."

"Have they stopped advancing?"

"Can't say for sure. I'll keep you posted." A pause. Shannon could hear Kirby speaking with someone else. When he was done he turned back to Shannon. "Shan, I think we need to try and stop this oil from going up Mosquito Pass, toward Westcott Bay and Roche Harbor. You know the rest. I just finished talking to the coordinator at the San Juan Oil Spill Association. We've got oil booms on the way from Roche Harbor and they should be here in half an hour."

"How soon 'til you can get them in place?"

SPILL

She could practically hear Kirby shrugging. He was fond of gestures when he spoke, even over long-distance communication. "The flood will start soon, so we need to move fast and utilize anybody who can help pronto. The real trick will be anchoring to the shore and sea bottom well enough to keep the tide from taking the boom away. I can get a couple of heavy-duty anchors to secure the middle section of the boom, but I suspect we'll also need to have a couple boats towing to keep it from running away in the strongest two or three hours of current during the big flood coming up. I'm sure most of the SOSA resources are employed around the freighter and the more northerly areas so…"

Shannon interjected, "Okay, I'll put out a call to volunteers to help coordinate with SOSA."

"Much obliged," Kirby said with a slight Southern drawl. "Oh, one other thing. Give the President of the Commercial Fishers Association a call and ask him if he can think of any way to mobilize his members to help, particularly with keeping oil off the beaches south of Mosquito Pass, like my front yard. I'm sure SOSA's got their hands full trying to contain all that oil around the ship and in booming off the top and bottom of Mosquito. Those fishermen may or may not be technically certified to respond, but when all is said and done, I doubt anybody's going to complain about who saves their beach from getting oiled and those Scandinavian fishermen are pretty darn resourceful."

Shannon rolled her eyes before putting out a general call. "Attention all vessels. This is Shannon Besser with the Whale Research Institute. We're looking for volunteers to help with containing an oil spill coming from a freighter grounding near Turn Point. Repeat, looking for volunteers to help in deploying and maintaining a containment boom to protect Mosquito Pass from the oil. There isn't much time, so please get back to me quickly if you're available."

A voice immediately answered, "This is Doug Anderson on the *Marianne*. We're…uh, we're a thirty-two-foot Bayliner coming down Mosquito Pass. Could we be of assistance?"

"Perfect," Shannon said. "Do you know where Andrew's Bay is? Can you get there from where you are?"

"Yes, ma'am."

"Head that way. There's a man named Kirby in an orange inflatable waiting there. He'll tell you what to do."

"Okay, I'll send my daughter, Sidney, ahead on her jet ski."

"Great. I'll keep you posted." As Shannon switched back to the general channel, she contemplated the wood grain in her desk. *Keep you posted*, she thought. *That's about all I can do right now.* Then she remembered Kirby's request to her call the President of the CFA. Shannon looked up his number and called. "Oly, this is Shannon over at the Whale Research Institute."

"Hi, Shan, goood tah hear yah voisa. Waasa oop?"

"Oly, we've got a serious emergency unfolding and thought maybe the fellows in your association might be able to help."

"Yah, shore, ya bet'cha. Vat cahn vee doo?"

"Well, I'm not really sure myself. A freighter hard grounded up at Turn Point with a couple hundred thousand gallons of bunker fuel that's spilling out and heading south with the tide. Kirby asked me to call you to see if you could think of anything you could do to keep it off the beaches down Kirby's way. I'd guess he's probably got Andrew's Bay and Open Bay in mind as one of the first vulnerable targets on the coming flood. He's working on a plan with the San Juan Oil Spill Association to try and keep it from going up Mosquito."

"Vell, let me tink." A pause. "I tink I goot goood ideyah. Vee fisermuns goot los uf coork lines. Maybe vee coould got suum cotton towols and lash dem to da coork linesa. Day vould absorb da oil maybe okay. Vat you tink?"

"Where are you going to get enough towels to do the job?"

"I gots lotsa friends. I call da churches, da service cluebs, da trift shopas, me fishermen friend's vifes. Day brung me anyting dat absorb ooil. Sleep baags, sheets, anyting dot caan git da ooil. Da fiskermens lash dem to fishnet coorklines fast as dey bring in absorbent stuff. We bring to Oopeen Baya fast wit' our boatsa already uppa dat vay. Okay. Oh, by dee vay, I gottsa vessal ofa oopurtuunaty ceertivecate training a few years back."

"Go for it, Oly. We've got nothing to lose."

"I call meh friends and gots vright to vork."

No sooner had she hung up than her Orca Network line buzzed.

"Hello, this is Shannon at Orca Network. We're kind of busy right now dealing with a serious emergency situation. If you're calling to report whales, we'll have to ask you to call back later."

The caller replied, "Oh, well, no I'm not calling about whales. My wife and two kids are in an emergency situation also, and I didn't know who else to call but thought maybe you could suggest who might help us. We were kayaking down the west side of Henry Island toward Limekiln Point to see the orcas. Just north of Kellett Bluff we encountered an oil slick. Thinking it would just be temporary, we kept going, but it only got worse and it closed in behind us as well. We're trapped, surrounded. We had to climb ashore to try to get out of the fumes. Now we're on a rock ledge on the outside of Henry Island about ten feet above the oily water."

Interrupting, Shannon said, "Yes, we know all about the source. A ship grounded at Turn Point. The ebb tide is carrying bunker fuel from the ship's ripped-open fuel tanks south along Henry Island."

"Well, we need help. We had to get out of our kayaks because we were overcome with nausea from the fumes. At least now our heads are off the water. It's still bad, but not nearly as much so. The rocks go straight up from where we are, so we can't go any higher. Can you think of any way we can get rescued? We called you because we had your whale sighting number and figured you might be in contact with whale watching boats or somebody who could help us."

Shannon replied, "I just might have a workable idea. There's a young lady with a jet ski not too far from you. Perhaps she could rescue one or two of you at a time. First, though, we need to get her parents' permission and some gas masks for her and your family. Let me make a call to the local oil spill folks and see if they have masks readily available. I've got your number, I'll get back shortly."

Shannon immediately called SOSA headquarters. The woman answering the phone said she thought the vehicle with the oil retention boom heading in that direction carried masks. She'd call the driver to check and call Shannon back immediately.

Shannon didn't need to wait long. The woman affirmed the possession of gas masks and said the rig would be near the shore at Hansbury Point in a few minutes.

Shannon responded, "Tell the boom delivery folks not to be surprised if a young lady on a jet ski comes by to borrow the masks." Then Shannon called Kirby. "Can you ask the young lady on the jet ski if she would be willing to mask up and help rescue a close-by family trapped by the oil, probably two at a time, if it's okay with her folks?"

Kirby replied, "She's coming up right now and I'll explain the situation to her. Assuming she's willing to help, I'll get her folks' contact info and talk to them."

———— ❧ ————

Sidney was more than willing. Even excited. Her dad, after being assured she'd have a mask and that the exposure time would be moderate, agreed to permit her to assist in such a necessary emergency rescue. Sidney immediately took off at full speed for the boom trailer to get the masks. After quickly beaching her jet ski, she ran up to the driver, who was already walking toward her with the masks in hand. He said, "Good luck, young lady. Sounds like quite a mission you're on."

He probably couldn't hear her "thanks," as she instantly turned and took off at a dead run to mount her jet ski.

Sidney quickly gunned her jet ski and was heading for Kellet Bluff at the south end of Henry Island.

As she rounded the point, she became engulfed in the oil. It was a strange sensation, as it dampened the vessel's usual high, wispy spray and rooster tail. It was only a couple more minutes before she spotted the kayaks and the family plastered up against the sheer rock wall. She idled up to the near vertical precipice the four were clinging to.

The dad shouted, "Thank God you're here! I can't believe how fast you got here. Take my wife and our little girl first."

Sidney lifted her mask and shouted back, "If you don't mind, sir, it will work out better for me weight-wise if I take your wife and son first. I may have trouble getting up on a plane with you and your heavier son at the same time."

"Oh, of course, I didn't think of that. My brain's probably a little fuzzy from all these nasty fumes. I suggested my daughter go first because she got very nauseous and looked like she was about to vomit from the fumes. However, she's much improved now."

"That's totally logical, sir. Now she's, what, ten feet off the water? We can talk about the physics of toxic fume concentrations in relation to the distance from the source later. For now I need to get you out of here pronto. You two hop on behind me."

Sidney tossed two masks over.

The mom and the older son donned them, stepped off a water-level rock, and jumped aboard the jet ski, with the son grabbing his mom's waist just as she grabbed on to Sidney's. Sidney yelled over the noise from the accelerating engine for them to hold on tight, as it was going to be a fast ride. She immediately fully rotated the speed controls in her right hand. It took what seemed to be an eternity to get up on a plane, but once she did, they were flying toward Kirby's inflatable just six or seven minutes away.

"Hey, Kirby, you're the closest sanctuary around, so here are a couple of passengers."

The two quickly jumped aboard Kirby's boat as Kirby shouted, "You're amazing. What's your name again?"

"Sidney...call me Sid. Talk to you later," she shouted through her mask. "The fumes are pretty bad up there, so I need to get the other two as quickly as possible."

Kirby said, "Of course," but Sidney blasted off before he could finish the last words.

In a few short minutes she was back to the two remaining stranded victims.

The dad yelled, "I tried to tie the kayaks to the rocks, but I'm not sure it will hold or what will happen as the tide changes."

Sidney replied, "Kayaks are tough. I'm sure we'll be able to find them in the next couple days, as there aren't any high winds forecasted. There sure won't be any boaters around here, so we don't have to worry about somebody thinking they found a couple of nice double kayaks."

Sidney handed them their masks, and they jumped on and were off, joining the rest of the family minutes later after the three-mile trip to Kirby's vessel.

The father commented, "Sure am glad to be free of those awful fumes. They can't be good for you."

Kirby answered, "You're quite right. The Exxon-Valdez spill workers who were exposed over a longer period of time haven't done well health-wise. Many have even died prematurely. Also, the orcas in Prince William Sound have done poorly. One genetically distinct subgroup hasn't had a birth in the intervening twenty-six years and will almost certainly go extinct. They of course surfaced and breathed air right at the water/air/oil interface where there's the greatest concentration of aerosol hydrocarbons. There's a proposal to ship vastly increased quantities of what's called bituminous crude down Haro Strait. The fumes you experienced coming off that barely refined bunker oil were bad enough, but mild compared to the bituminous oil. I need to get over to work on the oil boom to try and protect all the sensitive, pristine environs up Mosquito Pass. I'll drop you off there and you can catch a ride back to Roche with the boom transport people."

Sidney said, "Getting back to the oil fume concentrations you referenced standing on the rocks, you said the fumes weren't so bad once you were out of the kayaks and climbed ten feet or so off the water. That's totally logical and a great example of the physics/mathematics principles my honors math science teacher taught us. There's almost certainly an exponential inversely proportional relationship between the fume concentration and distance from the source. We've got a really cool teacher in my math and science courses. I just love it."

The dad said, "I'm an engineer, so I can understand the general principles you're espousing, but that must be quite a class he's teaching."

"He's a she," Sidney said with a twinkle in her eye.

———— ◦◦◦◦ ————

"Hey, Dad," Meagan said. She'd been watching the orcas from about a hundred yards away for fifteen minutes. Howard looked up to see what had taken her attention away from the orcas' show of popping their heads out of the water. A jet ski was throwing water high into the air as it passed by. "Isn't that Jason's girlfriend? She's awesome." Howard looked into his binoculars, instantly recognizing the long blonde hair, now streaming out from underneath a backward baseball cap. "Yes, I think it is." He waved his arms, much like Kirby had done to give the signal. At first he thought she might keep going without noticing, but the jet ski did a quick right-angle turn and came their way. "Sidney," Howard said, lifting his voice conspicuously. "Fancy meeting you out here."

"Oh, hey, Mr. Strander."

The entire ship fairly rocked as Jason came tearing from the cabin. "Hey, Sidney."

Sidney smiled shyly. "Hey, Jason. Look, I don't know if you know yet, but—"

"The spill," Howard interrupted. "Yeah, we know."

"I'm heading to shore to see what kind of help I might be."

"I'll come with you." Jason was halfway over the railing already.

"Hold it," Howard said.

"Come on, Dad. You don't need me to help with the speakers. You've got Meagan and Mom to help. Besides, you can see the orcas have turned and we're probably pretty much done here." He looked up with pleading eyes. "Please?"

Howard sighed. "Okay. But be careful. Sidney, do you have a cellphone?"

"Yes, Mr. Strander."

"Jason, leave yours with us. We need a spare more than you need yours. Besides, you could easily lose it or drop it. Use Sidney's waterproof one to give us a call, okay? Keep us in the loop."

It spoke volumes that Jason handed his phone over without complaint, hopping on the back of the jet ski and wrapping his arms around Sidney's waist. Perhaps it was just an excuse to be near her, at first, but as soon as the jet ski took off, Howard could tell by the look on his face that he was actually clinging for dear life now. They roared away.

Chapter 9

Kirby could see the trucks carrying boom material from his boat as he idled close to the shore, searching for a good area to launch the booms. SOSA's booms had arrived with a handful of trained SOSA volunteers dressed in luminescent orange jackets. As four men filed out of the first of the three heavy-duty, extended-cabs, four-wheel-drive pickups pulling the boom trailers, Kirby beached his craft roughly perpendicular to the trucks idling on the county road about a football field away. Kirby and the rescued kayak family jumped out of the boat onto the sandy beach. The owner of the nearest home approached Kirby and asked, "What's happening, partner?"

Kirby began to introduce himself.

The man stopped him saying, "Heck, everybody knows who you are...the whale guy, Kirby Jackson. We see you going by here all the time. So what brings you in this close today?"

Kirby replied, "Its not good news. That's for sure. There's been a significant oil spill up on Stuart Island and it's headed this way when the tide turns. We're looking for the best site to place and maintain a boom so the oil doesn't go by here to the north, up Mosquito, into Wescott Bay, Roche...you know all the places...on the flood."

The homeowner replied, "I was just watching a report of that spill on TV. I thought all the oil was on the other side of Henry Island."

"It is now, but there's a northwesterly pushing it to the southeast. That, along with the normal current pattern, is guaranteed to bring it right by here unless we can stop it with those booms on the trailers over there." He pointed in the rig's direction.

"What can I do to help?" the homeowner asked.

"If this is your property, with your permission, it would be an ideal place to launch the boom. Would it be okay to bring the rig across your yard to the shoreline?"

"Heck yes. I sure don't want any of that oil going by my place. Tell them to drive on over."

Kirby signaled the truck driver to back the rig up toward him. Kirby spotted while the driver navigated the trailer to the water's edge, stopping him when the back tires touched the water. The driver hopped out. He and Kirby flung open the trailer's back gate and began unspooling yards and yards of boom material, kept afloat by a thick rung of buoyant rubber. Getting it started into the water while trying to keep it untangled and in place was like wrestling a giant python. There were hundreds of yards of the material to be pulled off the reel, and two more trailers behind waiting with similar cargos.

Kirby paused to wipe his brow when the whine of an approaching motor caused him to look out over the water. It was Sidney wearing her reversed cap. A slender boy in swim trunks was on the back seat of the Jet Ski with both arms wrapped snugly around her waist. They were headed straight for shore, with nary a sign of slowing down. Kirby waded out into the water up to his knees, trying to grab their attention, warn her to slow down, but she either didn't see or ignored him, because she came in fast, breaking over the shallow waves. Kirby winced and waited for impact.

At the last possible moment, she pulled back on the handles, bringing the Jet Ski in at a sharp angle that threw up a wall of water. At a more reasonable pace, the machine came aground, churning up the sandy beach underneath.

Kirby now recognized the boy as Howard's son from the sailboat. He and Sidney dismounted almost without having to get their feet wet, although the boy stumbled on rubbery legs, wearing a face that suggested he hadn't expected Sidney to pull a stunt like that.

"I told you," Sidney laughed. "My jet ski is amphibious."

"I thought you meant, like, it was frog-friendly."

"No, silly. Amphibious means—"

Kirby waded over to them, feeling rather annoyed now that the Jet Ski's waves had gotten his pant legs wet. "Sorry, Sid," he called, "there's no pleasure boating allowed at the moment. You can see —"

She interrupted, "We're here to see if we can be of help. My dad said you might need assistance."

"Right, right," Kirby said, "You've already proven yourself with me. You're just in time. We're going to need lots of help to pull this off." He waved towards the boom, where the driver of the first trailer had finished pulling the first of the boom material off the reel, into the water. "We could certainly use someone with your motoring skills, Sid. We were expecting a boat to come by and help tow the boom, but you're already here and we need to get the boom tied off on the Henry Island shore before the flood current starts."

Sidney tipped her hat back. "Just tell us what to do."

"We're going to start rolling out the boom, here, to block the oil from going up the pass here at the narrowest spot. We're going to tie one end just over there on Hansbury Point." He pointed a short way down the beach. "If you can tow it across and find somewhere to tie off... across the way, over there on Henry, and help anchor it..."

Sidney nodded and turned to Jason. "I'll drive. Do you think you can keep track of and hold onto the end of the boom?"

Jason nodded unconvincingly.

"It might be tricky finding things on shore to tie off to," Kirby said.

"We'll find something," Jason said with newfound conviction as his face regained its color, seeming to have recovered from his harrowing ride over.

Kirby handed Jason a loop he'd tied in the rope coming from the end of the boom. As Sidney motored away from the shore, they came to the end of the slack, which pulled the Jet Ski's stern a few inches deeper into the water. Jason held onto the boom end with one hand and anchored the other arm around

Sidney's firm waist. She in turn held tight to the handle bars, to prevent the strain of the boom from pulling both of them into the water. Sidney began towing at a steady pace towards Henry Island.

∽∽∽

The boom was such a bright orange that Jason suspected it would glow in the dark. It was also heavy and threatened to slide out of his hands. Sidney kept a steady line towards the island across the way. It was a bit mesmerizing, the way the orange boom bobbed in the prop wash of their jet ski. A strip of rubberized material hung down a couple feet from the buoyant boom to create a barrier.

There wasn't any oil yet, but Jason would occasionally look up from his work to make sure. Other than that, he concentrated on his task, so hard that he nearly fell over each time he tried to adjust his hold around Sidney.

"Check it out," she cried over the roar of the engine. "We're on the news." She pointed upwards with one hand as a seaplane with a big number five stenciled on the underbelly flew overhead. They were so low; Jason could actually see the reporter and cameraman inside.

"Think they're here to cover the oil spill?"

"No, they're following a hot story on delinquent teens on jet skis."

Jason had to look at her face to make sure she was teasing. The ends of her long blonde hair whipped about in the wind.

As they pulled up to the shore on Henry Island, Sidney gently throttled the craft onto the rocky beach. The beach was hardly five feet wide, cut off by a bank jutting upwards. A grove of stubborn trees grew along the bank top, their roots digging down through the rock, some even breaking through to dangle in thin air.

Jason held the end of the line. Kirby had been right. There weren't many places to tie the other end.

After Sidney beached the Jet Ski and hopped off, her sandals crunched the pebbles and bits of broken shell underfoot as she paced back and forth, neck craned upwards. At last, she found what she was looking for. "Jason, pull the boom over here."

Pulling with everything he had brought him to her side.

She was inspecting a sturdy tree limb. It looked strong enough to do the job, if they could reach it.

"Give me a lift," she said.

He looked at her, not understanding.

"If I stand on your shoulders, I can reach it."

"Oh, right."

He knelt down as she kicked off her sandals. The soles of her feet were rough and callused as she planted them on his shoulders, but her skin was soft and smooth where he gripped one of her ankles to support her. "Ready?" he asked. "On the count of three."

"Three!" they both said together, and Jason launched her into the air.

With their combined height, Sidney could reach the branch. She wasn't heavy at all, but Jason hoped she would be quick. His palms were beginning to get sweaty, and he didn't know how much longer he could support her and hold onto the boom rope.

"Jason, hand me the end of the rope." Her hands moved quickly for only a brief moment. "There!" she cried triumphantly, having looped three half-hitches around the sturdy stub of a broken limb as if in a calf-roping competition.

He helped her down, extending his hand for her to take as she hopped off. If she noticed his palms were sweaty, she didn't say anything.

"Think that will hold?" he asked.

"Those are three genuine half-hitches. They're not going anyplace," she said with a decisive nod. "My dad taught me how to tie knots. They turned to watch how the tide was already beginning to reshape the straight line they'd made across the water with the boom into a "U" shape.

"I don't think there's much we can do about that current," Jason observed.

Sidney drew her lips tight. "Yeah, that's up to Kirby and his SOSA buddies to deal with." She gave an aggravated little huff, slumping her shoulders, before heading back to the Jet Ski. "Come on. Let's see if there's any more for us to do."

As they headed back towards Hansbury Point, Jason felt his stomach drop, and not just because Sidney was going at don't-ask-how-fast miles per hour. A line of shiny black had appeared on the surface. The oil had made its appearance.

It was spreading, coming their way. Jason could smell it, like newly laid asphalt. It moved like an amoeba, spreading its tendrils out, seeking anything to surround and swallow. And there, near the oil's leading edge, something else was moving, too quickly and sporadically to be the oil itself. Jason wished he'd taken a pair of binoculars from the *Serendipity*, but he had to make do with shielding his eyes against the sun.

"Sidney! There's a bird!"

The jet ski rode its own wake as the motor idled. Standing still, it was easier to see the telltale flapping of wings as the incapacitated bird tried in vain to fly. It was so thoroughly covered in oil, it was impossible to tell what kind of bird it was.

"We can't just leave it there," Jason said.

Sidney didn't say anything. With a determined lift in her chin, she spun the Jet Ski around and hit the throttle. As they sped towards the oil, Jason mused at how crazy this was, heading straight into the thick of things—literally. Surely his parents wouldn't approve. Good thing they weren't here.

"Get ready to grab it," Sidney called over her shoulder.

"Grab it? Like, with my bare hands?"

"Here's a towel." She reached under her seat and handed him a threadbare, ratty, white hand towel.

"Well then," he deadpanned, "that's so much better."

He took the towel, half-expecting it to dissolve in his hands. He lowered himself onto the back step and leaned over as far as he dared, gripping the seat loop. They pulled up alongside the struggling bird, and Jason made a grab for it. Unfortunately, this only spooked the animal, and it beat its wings at them with renewed efforts.

"Can you get any closer?"

"I'll try," Sidney said doubtfully.

She spun a quick one-eighty, which brought them so close to the edge that the oil lapped against the side of their vessel. Jason tried again.

"Come on, fella, it's okay, it's going to be okay," he mumbled in a steady string of consoling words as he tried to get closer. The bird would not be wrangled though. There was nothing else to do. Jason took a deep breath and lunged.

SPILL

The entire Jet Ski listed to one side, and Sidney gave a yelp before leaning hard to the other side to steady it. Jason felt himself lifting up and outwards, and then he was over the oily water. He was going in. There was no helping it.

A hand grabbed him by his trunks. He hung suspended for a few seconds before Sidney yelled, "Hurry up! I can't hold you forever."

He obliged, grabbing the bird so quickly it didn't have time for protest. With a hand on either wing and a thin layer of towel between skin and feather, he hauled the bird up as Sidney hauled him back.

He fell heavily into his seat with a mass of sticky, tarry bird struggling in his lap. The thing was strong. It took all his strength to keep the wings from unfurling, but that didn't keep the bird from kicking out with its pink, webbed, but deceptively clawed feet. Oil seeped through the towel onto his hands, arms, shirt, swimming trunks, legs, even dripping down onto his feet. He turned his head away so as not to get any in his mouth.

Now it was his time to yell, "Hurry! I don't know how long I can hold on."

Sidney didn't need to be told twice. She kicked the jet ski into high gear and tore off for Roche, where they'd heard a cleaning center was being set up, with their belligerent bundle in tow.

Chapter 10

Michelle glanced once more into her compact mirror and took one last moment to pat down her hair. The winds were picking up, which didn't bode well for the task at hand.

"Ready, Ms. Kurosawa?" the cameraman asked.

She nodded and slipped her compact into the front pocket of her blazer, taking up her microphone instead. The cameraman gave her the signal, counting down from three with his fingers.

"Michelle Kurosawa here," she said into the camera with her usual professional flare. "I'm coming to you live from San Juan Island, where a shipping accident has left Haro Strait exposed to an oil spill that some are calling the worst environmental disaster Puget Sound has ever seen. If you look behind me here"—she waved her arm, and the cameraman panned to the *Bel Amica*, caught on the rocks of Turn Point behind them—"you can see where the ship in question has run aground. So far, clean-up attempts have proved largely unsuccessful. Even under ideal circumstances, the people out here helping with the clean-up can hope to collect only twenty to forty percent of the spill within the next forty-eight hours."

A gust of wind blew through, and from behind, the shouts of the men and women working frantically on the ship could be heard, even on the camera, Michelle suspected.

"Initial reports from the Coast Guard indicate the crew and the captain showed no signs of intoxication or fatigue, but the captain has not returned our calls as of this time. We'll keep you posted as this story progresses. Back to you, Tom."

"Thanks, Michelle," the anchorman back at the station said into her earpiece.

As he launched into the next story, the cameraman lowered his camera and gave her the sign that the broadcast had been cut. Michelle sighed in relief and let her microphone arm relax. "Okay, that was good," she said. "Be sure to get some shots of the ship for the evening news. And go ahead and interview anyone who's willing to talk." She straightened out her blazer and squared her shoulders as she began to walk away.

"Where are you going?" the cameraman asked.

"I'm going to see if I can convince the captain to speak with us," she said over her shoulder. The wind carried away the next part. "Think of what a great exclusive would be."

———

"Hey, you there, Shannon?" Howard said into the radio as Meagan continued to monitor the speakers. "Howard Strander again. Hope I'm not distracting you with all these calls or anything."

"No, no, you're fine," Shannon said. She had a calming voice. If she weren't already employed with this whale outfit, Howard would have suggested she seek a job as a 911 dispatch operator. "What's up?"

"Just wanted to keep up-to-date. We've been at it for about an hour now and…as far as I can tell, things look good. Everything good on your end?"

"The clean-up's going pretty slow," Shannon said bluntly. "They're assessing the damage right now. Any news on the whales?"

"They've retreated…a little."

"That's great news."

Howard sighed and ran a hand over his face. "What do we do now?"

"They're amassing volunteers on shore," Shannon said levelly. "Setting up clean-up stations for animals, maintaining the boom, that sort of thing."

"What about the ship? What's going to happen to it?"

"The Coast Guard will figure something out. Last I heard, the boom they'd set up had failed, so it's still leaking oil pretty heavily. They'll probably try as best they can to patch it up, but..." She paused. Howard wondered what sort of gesture went along with that: a shrug, a shake of the head? "You don't need to worry about *that*. You're doing good work where you are."

Howard didn't *feel* like he was doing good work. Rather, it felt like he was bumbling around, trying to make up for this whole thing. *It's all my fault*, he thought. *I should have been more careful. It's all my fault.*

"Jesus, kid, what happened to you?"

Jason hopped off the jet ski, holding the bird out towards the volunteer who'd come running as soon as they'd beached. The bird had been struggling so hard on the trip to the treatment facility that now it appeared spent and hardly struggled at all.

The volunteer had elbow-length rubber gloves on and a surgical mask, so Jason couldn't even tell what he looked like except that he wore glasses under a pair of goggles. The volunteer took the mess from Jason and tucked the bird firmly against his heavy rubber apron. "If you haven't been trained for it," he admonished, "you really shouldn't be handling these animals at all. I don't suppose either of you passed the required seven-hour hazmat training program, hmm?"

Sidney and Jason shook their heads.

The volunteer sighed behind his mask. "It's done now. Just don't do it again." He jerked his head for them to come along.

Sidney and Jason followed him to the tent where stacks of cages and plastic bins had been set up—Jason hobbled, as his oil-slickened clothing was beginning to become heavy and uncomfortable to move in.

"We need to get this little guy warmed up." The volunteer took a blanket out of one of the bins and wrapped it around the bird, who was too exhausted to fight back. The volunteer rubbed the bird down, moving his hands in circular motions that generated heat but didn't do much to remove the oil. Jason expected him to start the cleaning right away, but instead the volunteer put the bird and blanket in an empty cage. "They need time to stabilize before we can begin cleaning them," he explained. "We'll see if he's thirsty or hungry after he's calmed down a little bit. As for you…"

Jason thought maybe his mom could take a lesson in disapproving tone from this guy.

"We need to get you to the hazmat shower. Come on."

He led them a little way up the beach, where something like a bright yellow kiddie swimming pool had been set up. Another man in similar gear—apron, gloves, mask—took one look at Jason and motioned for him to step into the kiddie pool. He felt acutely aware of Sidney watching him when the hazmat guy said, "You need to get out of those clothes, kid, if we're ever going to get you clean."

Fortunately, the volunteer took that moment to tap Sidney's shoulder and draw her attention away. He whispered something into her ear and she nodded. "Jason, I'm going to go call your folks and tell them we're okay!" she called over her shoulder as the volunteer led her away.

Jason sighed in relief and began pulling his sticky clothes off, no easy feat. His shirt wanted to cling to his skin, and whenever his fingers touched the black substance, it stuck and would not shake off. It was like trying to get glue off. It took longer than it should have to get everything but his shorts off, and the hazmat guy collected the ruined clothes into a biohazard bag.

Then came the hose to clean the rest of him off. Jason was doubly glad Sidney wasn't around to hear his yelp of surprise as the barely lukewarm water crashed against him.

———⊗⊗⊗———

"Look at this mess," Doug Anderson sighed as he looked over the side of the *Marianne*. Oily debris islands had begun to build up, giant blobs of kelp, sticks, pop weed, and whatever else got caught up in the swirling currents of riptide. And the tide was increasing in intensity. About an hour after Sidney had left on the jet ski, an especially large pool of oil and debris had built up behind the boom, along with the bodies of birds—some still alive, others drowned or suffocated—drifting along the surface, leaving tarry feathers in their wake.

It was hard not to retrieve them.

"Doug, honey." Tanya came running from the cabin. "Sidney's on the line. She says she's fine. She picked up the Strander boy—remember, the family from Roche Harbor?—and they're doing what they can to help with the booms and an oiled bird." She glanced over his shoulder at the struggling birds in the water. "There has to be something we can do," she said.

"We really should leave the people with the knowledge and facilities to deal with it."

A loon squawked in misery. He could only tell it was a loon from the familiar call alone; the bird looked like any of the others, hardly even distinguishable from the corpses around it. Tanya gave a defeated sigh that broke into a little sob. And that little sob broke Doug.

"Get the net," he said.

Tanya looked up at him, uncomprehending.

"The net," he reiterated. "The fishing net. It should still be below deck."

Tanya caught his meaning and fairly flung herself down the stairs to fetch the net.

"The one that extends," he called after her. Meanwhile, he rummaged through the storage, sorting through life jackets and boat bumpers until he found what he was looking for. The old tarp hadn't seen much use in recent years—it was covered in dust and spider webs—but it would do to keep him from having a "spill" of his own on his deck carpet.

Tanya returned, extending the fishing net's handle out as far as it would go.

Doug sat at the helm and approached the boom carefully, navigating against the strong tide as he moved into position expertly. Tanya leaned out over the bow and scooped the exhausted loon off the oily debris pile. Its little body was completely slack as she brought it up and over the edge, dumping it as gently as she could manage onto the tarp.

"Sidney says they have a station set up for the oiled animals back at Roche Harbor," she called as she tried again for another bird. By the time they headed to shore, they had three barely-alive birds on the deck of their boat, and only then after sifting through something like six bodies to get to them. Tanya paced around the outside of the tarp, fretting the entire way.

It turned out they weren't the only good Samaritans. At Roche Harbor, the rescue and cleaning station was working on dozens of birds as more were brought in, mostly by boaters like themselves. Two river otters and several harbor seals were also being tended to, wrapped in blankets to keep up their warmth. They were being hydrated using baby bottles and stomach tubes. It looked to be a time-consuming enterprise, but dozens of volunteers of all ages were staffing the operation, led by SOSA-trained staff.

The Andersons hauled the tarp up onto the beach, leaving very little mess in their wake. All the while, the birds kept looking up at them with their sad little eyes, the only parts of them not covered in oil.

"Will you be able to save them?" Tanya asked the volunteer who came out to help them with their load.

"We'll see," she said. "These guys were lucky you were there for them."

Doug looked down at them. If these were the lucky ones, he shuddered to think of the unlucky ones.

———— ∞ ————

"Mr. Petrakis! Mr. Petrakis!"

Captain Petrakis lifted his head at the horrible mangling of his name to find an Asian woman in a business dress suit waving at him. In one hand she had a microphone emblazoned with the numeral five on it. She was with the press.

He grumbled a few curses under his breath and popped the collar of his jacket, as if he could keep her away as easily as a light rain. She was persistent, though, and pushed her way through the surveying team. She had a hard time of it, as nobody wanted to make room for her.

"George Petrakis!" she called again.

"Yor-go," he corrected. "Peh-*tray*-kiss."

"That's you?" She struggled her way next to him, slightly breathless. "You're the captain of the *Bel Amica?*"

"No press."

"You don't have a statement you want to give?"

He looked her in the eyes, and she looked straight back, albeit craning her neck upwards a bit. "I will talk," he said slowly, deliberately, "only in private."

"That can be arranged."

"Give me time to prepare."

She continued to meet his gaze. "Sure."

"I will talk to you in…" He had to consider the amount of time to tell her. It had to be enough. "Two hours," he decided at last. "I talk only to you."

"Do you agree to be filmed?"

He waved her question away. "Yes, yes, is fine, but give me two hours. Meet in private."

"Where would you like to meet?"

He could have laughed at the earnestness in her voice. Instead, he kept it to himself as he pretended to consider. Finally, he stretched his hand out over the side of the cliff, pointing to the outlook of Turn Point. "There."

She seemed satisfied and wormed her way out of the crowd again.

Once she was gone, Petrakis sighed in relief. Now he only had to make sure he was gone within two hours.

Chapter 11

Kirby wondered what they'd put on his banner. "You know," he'd said when he'd voiced his concern to Shannon and Jack, "the little banner they put at the bottom of the screen whenever they interview anyone? Like, 'Whale Watcher' or 'Princeton Graduate.'"

"Or 'Military Drop-Out Turned Foremost Whale Expert,'" Shannon suggested.

"I think I'd prefer 'Super Genius' myself," Kirby chuckled back. "But we'll deal with that later. Right now I've got to give the blamed interview, right?" He straightened the buttons of his shirt. "Knew I should have worn something better today."

"You look fine," Shannon tsk'd.

"But still, Cooper Andrews?" Jack let out a long, low whistle. "This lady guaranteed you a meeting with *the* Cooper Andrews?"

"That's what she said. I've still got reservations. It's not that I distrust the press, but rather that I mistrust their motives at times. She said he was flying out here right now to do the interview in person. How's that for VIP treatment, eh?"

"But you've got to do this one first with the local gal?"

Kirby nodded then turned away from the mirror. He might not exactly cut an impressive figure with his button-down shirt and khakis, and he hadn't had a shower since this thing began, but it would have to do.

The petite woman from Channel Five News had been hounding him for details on the story. She and her crew were waiting at Turn Point for Kirby as he took his time coming over the path from Prevost. It was normally a scenic view, one of the very best the islands had to offer. Now, however, the scent of oil hung heavy in the air, irritating the lungs and eyes. Oil-tainted waves below broke upon saltwater flora and fauna that clung to the shoreline rocks.

"Michele Kurosawa," she said, giving him a firm and overly friendly handshake, which he couldn't hope to return in all its intensity. "Thank you for taking time to speak with us. We know you're very busy."

"Honestly, there's not much else to be done, now that night's setting in." Kirby looked out to the west toward Turn Point, where the sun was beginning to set, casting pale pink against the clouds.

"Yes, let's do this while we still have some daylight." The reporter snapped her fingers and the cameraman hefted his camera onto his shoulder, pointing it at Kirby. The woman came up to about his chin as she thrust her microphone in his face. The cameraman counted down on silent fingers, and then the woman launched into an introduction Kirby had heard many times before on the local news channel. "Michele Kurosawa here, speaking with whale expert Kirby Jackson. Mr. Jackson, what can you tell us about the accident?"

"Right now the spill stretches about one mile by five miles," Kirby began. "We have estimates that about two hundred thousand gallons of bunker fuel have been released into area waters. I did the math. That's the equivalent to having one gallon of oil in your thirty-by-thirty-five-foot swimming pool, or two tablespoons in your bathtub. Neither of which you'd want to swim in."

"How are clean-up efforts coming along?" Ms. Kurosawa asked.

"As well as can be expected." Kirby gave a helpless shrug. "Under ideal circumstances, we'd be able to pick up about…eighty thousand gallons, or about forty percent of what's been put out in the first forty-eight hours, but as you can see, with the winds and the tides, these are hardly ideal conditions, but pretty typical. The recovery number is much, much lower in reality, but we're still out here doing what we can."

"What does the situation look like going forward?"

"We'll see what it's like in the morning. The oil will be a lot less concentrated tomorrow on the flood. Some will have evaporated, some will be skimmed, and mostly it will just have dispersed over a wider area or hit the shoreline. "

Ms. Kurosawa stared at him blankly. He could see little of this meant anything to her.

"And the ship?" she asked.

"Well...uh, you'd have to check with the Coast Guard about that." Kirby scratched the back of his neck. "She'll probably need to get rid of some of her freight to lighten her as much as possible." He considered the wreck below them, the way the ship had been slammed high and dry against the rocks. "She grounded on a fairly high tide and will need to come off on a high tide. They'll probably need to use small, very accurately targeted explosive charges to blast away however much of that impaling rock they can get on her port side. I'd bet she won't be loading anything again. She'll probably be scrapped."

"So," Ms. Kurosawa went on, despite the fact that they had traveled outside his area of expertise, "it's a Panamanian-registry vessel, owned by a Greek national, in U.S. waters heading to unload in Canada. That's quite the international conundrum. One of the big questions people are already fretting over is who's responsible for all this."

"I couldn't tell you," Kirby answered honestly.

When it became obvious he was not going to elaborate, Ms. Kurosawa took her microphone back and spoke into the camera. "There are no easy answers to be had here tonight, but that's not dampening the spirit of the brave volunteers working to get this situation under control. As always, I'm Michele Kurosawa, and we'll be following this story as it develops. Back to you, Tom."

Kirby had turned quickly to walk away as Ms. Kurosawa hollered his way, "Thanks, Mr. Jackson. You were very informative. Now stay tuned, folks. We have some important interviews coming up when we come back."

———∞∞∞———

Ms. Kurosawa retrieved her compact from her blazer pocket, looked into its mirror, and made minor adjustments to her lipstick. She put the compact back as she motioned for Coast Guard Captain Smith to step forward and join her. The cameraman maneuvered to line up the shot of the wounded ship with Haro Strait and distant Vancouver Island in the background. The cameraman held up three …two…one finger.

"We're very fortunate to have the Coast Guard's Captain Smith join us now to provide more information on the plans to refloat the freighter. Thank you for joining us, Captain. Could you give us a timeline for refloating this wounded vessel?"

"Ma'am, we will attempt to refloat this vessel day after tomorrow on the highest tide of the month. To prepare for that, we have removed as many container units as we could. Not an easy thing to do under these circumstances. We've only been able to get about half of them. Of equal importance, we've removed as much of the pinnacle impaling the port bottom as possible. That was a very delicate task. Our contractor used strategically placed explosive charges to chip away at that granite rock. They had to be careful because a too powerful or misplaced charge could have further damaged the hull or some of the remaining containers. We have reason to believe there may be some container cargo in an unknown location that would be dangerous if jostled or concussed by either the pinnacle removal or the ungrounding. Possibly even explosive. We tried to further remove more of the rock with an underwater jackhammer, but the tide was too strong for the diver to manage the hammer."

"That's very interesting. What's the cargo you're worried about?"

"I can't tell you more about that. Chances are there won't be any problems. Most likely the cargo isn't hazardous or it's far enough from any jostling to be okay."

"Thank you very much, Captain Smith."

"You're welcome, ma'am."

The cameraman indicated they had gone to commercials. "Five minutes, Ms. Kurosawa."

She took a deep breath and looked around. Petrakis was running late. If he didn't get here soon, they'd have to do the interview live. Which was fine, live coverage made for better news, but it made her nervous that he hadn't shown up yet. Michele Kurosawa had a nose for this sort of thing, and she smelled a rat.

She stood on the bluff and scanned the area, doing a slow and thorough one-eighty. A seaplane swooped in from overhead and taxied to the shoreline in the lee of the freighter. It struck Kurosawa as odd, seeing as most of the back-and-forth traffic had died off for the day. She watched as it kept its engine running and neared the shore. That's when she saw him: Captain Petrakis, briefcase in hand, was hailing a ride.

"Captain Petrakis!" she called down.

If he heard, he ignored her.

"I can't believe this," she muttered, at the same time feeling a sense of excitement. A new development in the story. The captain of the downed freighter was attempting to flee the scene. She jabbed her cameraman. "Over here, get lots of footage," she said as Captain Petrakis stepped onto the pontoon of the seaplane. "Captain Smith!"

Petrakis might be ignoring her, but Captain Smith, who had started back down to his waiting launch, turned at her call.

She pointed towards the seaplane. "Is Captain Petrakis authorized to leave the area?"

Smith seemed confused for a moment, then he followed her pointing finger towards the seaplane. He drew his brows together and squared his shoulders. "No, ma'am, absolutely not."

<hr />

In fact, Captain Smith could confirm that Petrakis had firm orders not to leave the ship or the immediate area until the actual ungrounding attempt began. Something fishy was going on, and Smith needed to put his people on it. As he hurried down the rocky knoll toward the seaplane, he pulled his portable VHF from his jacket pocket. "Captain Smith to Seaman Anders."

"Sir, Seaman Anders back."

"Go order Captain Petrakis not to board that seaplane." If suspicion proved correct, Petrakis would need more than just a friendly reminder of his standing orders.

Captain Smith's cutter pulled up next to the seaplane just as he arrived back at the shoreline. He jumped onto the plane's port pontoon and, in quick succession, grabbed the cross member, swung to the starboard pontoon, grabbed the cutter's rail, and pulled himself up and over the rail onto the deck.

"Cut those engines," he shouted over the plane's engine noise. "Captain Petrakis, throw your briefcase up here and come aboard my vessel immediately."

Petrakis, with far less athleticism and even less enthusiasm, complied. At that very instant, his cell pinged. The taller Captain Smith, standing next to him, read the text over Petrakis's shoulder: *Are you in the air heading to the Sidney airport yet?*

"What the hell's going on here?" he asked, pointing to the phone. "Under the law derived from the National Oil and Hazardous Substance Pollution Contingency Plan, the Coast Guard ordered you to stay aboard your vessel or in the immediate vicinity."

"Sir, I fly to Sidney to find motel," Petrakis said. "I must have good sleep, a meal, and shower."

"Captain, you have good sleeping quarters aboard your vessel. The Coast Guard is supplying you with the same three squares I've been eating, and if you need a shower that badly, it certainly would have been provided aboard my vessel. With all due respect, I'm not sure you're shooting straight."

"'Shooting straight?' What means? I've not shot anybody."

"It means I don't think you're being honest with me. I think you're trying to make a run for it."

"Run for it? I no understand."

"You're trying to skip out on us. Leave. Take off. Open your briefcase and let me have a look inside."

"Uh, well…" Petrakis gripped the briefcase to his chest. "I needed money for airplane ride and motel. Only a little."

"Let's have a look inside."

"Okay, okay." He complied reluctantly.

"That's only a 'little' money? There must be thousands in there," Captain Smith asserted.

"Only to keep safe."

"You expect me to believe that kind of cash would be safer in a briefcase going through customs than in your vessel's safe? What are those other papers?"

"Just documents."

"Let's have a look." Captain Smith picked up two official-appearing documents. "This is the vessel documentation and here's the registration. Why would you take these?" Picking up another piece with scribbling on it, he read, "7:00 p.m. seaplane to Sidney...8:00 p.m. flight 345 Sidney to Vancouver...10:00 p.m. flight 873 Vancouver to Amsterdam...Amsterdam to Athens... Captain Petrakis, under laws establishing Coast Guard authority in spill incidents; I am placing you under arrest for lying and impeding an investigation. Now, I'm going to ask you some additional questions, and I suggest you answer truthfully or you will be in even more trouble."

"Captain, I'm sorry I lie," Petrakis said, his English suddenly improving. "My company order me fly home. They make schedule and order I take papers for ownership of boat. They say take or destroy ship log entries that show rudder problems. I told them to fix problem. They no listen."

"That's better. If you had come clean when I first asked, I could have avoided arresting you."

"I'm sorry, captain."

"Me too," Smith muttered as Seaman Anders escorted him below deck.

Turning to channel sixty-eight, Shannon announced, "Well, folks, it looks like we're calling it a night. Good job, everyone. Take a break and we'll see you here again at 9:00 a.m. tomorrow if you can continue helping."

"Kirby," Jack broke in, "do you think we need to do any towing of the boom on the smallish ebb and flood between now and then?"

Kirby came on, and Shannon felt like she was back on one of those party lines they'd had when she was in high school.

"Naw," Kirby replied. "Those tides are small enough that I think our shore ties and mid-channel boom anchors will do the trick holding the boom in place. But maybe we should have someone check on them periodically."

Howard Strander, from the *Serendipity*, came in. "I can do that," he said. "You have lots of other things to do. And if it does look like there is some need to tow on it again, I think, between my sailboat and Sidney's Jet Ski, we can handle it. That will give you guys a chance to monitor the whales. If we do need help or advice, we can always call."

"Great," Kirby said. "The tide is starting to slack up now. The small flood starts about 3:00 a.m. If you don't mind staying up..."

"It's the least I can do," Howard said.

As she listened, Shannon wanted to tell him that he didn't need to take the burden of this entire thing on himself. She wanted to tell him that human error made accidents like this inevitable and that he shouldn't beat himself up over it. But she also knew that hardly anything she could say would relieve the poor man's guilt.

"I'll let your son know he's relieved for now, but if we could keep him and the other girl on standby around 4:00..."

"I'm sure he'll be amenable," Howard answered.

Shannon thanked him again and switched over to a private channel to speak with Jack and Kirby.

"How are things going with the skimmer?" she asked.

Kirby answered. "Skimming that small percentage of the oil that was nicely concentrated next to the boom around the freighter was going smoothly until the operator hit a patch of jetsam with small sticks. He couldn't touch that with the skimmer, so a good...I'd say eighty percent of the oil was left in those debris islands, hit a beach, or was dispersed. I'd have to call the skimming's overall effect negligible."

"When we were living up in Alaska," Jack said, "the same problem plagued clean-up efforts in Prince William Sound after the Exxon-Valdez spill. The skimmers were continually plugged up by debris."

"So..." Shannon approached the topic slowly. "I guess the question for tomorrow will be whether to use dispersants or not."

"Shan," Kirby sighed, "you know those chemicals cause more harm than good."

"The industry folks will want to use them," Jack pointed out. "Out of sight, out of mind, that sort of thing."

"We'll need to talk them out of it, then," Kirby came back snappishly, even if Jack was only playing devil's advocate. "I've got tons of research under my belt that shows those chemicals harm microorganisms in the water column and affect the whole food chain adversely."

"I know, I know," Jack was quick to agree.

Shannon jumped in to cool rising tempers. "Leave that to us, Kirby. PR's more our thing anyway. You just worry about clean-up, the boom, and keeping those whales at bay."

She could audibly hear Kirby relax and couldn't blame him for getting so worked up. The man had a passion for whales that few people could truly appreciate, and after years of having grant money categorically denied to him based on his anti-sonar stance, he still remained the whales' number one advocate. The Navy would gladly give him fistfuls of money if only he'd keep his mouth shut about the harmful, often lethal, effects their sonar had on marine mammals, and whales in particular, but Kirby could not set his conscience aside in the name of compromise. And his stubbornness was one of his more endearing traits, even if it caused him to bump heads with others at times.

"Get some sleep, Kirby," Shannon finished. "I think we've all earned a little rest."

<hr />

Sidney dropped Jason off at 9:00 p.m., just as the last light from the sun was peeking out over the black shape of Vancouver Island. She took off and motored back over the boom toward the *Marianne*, anchored in four fathoms just south of the entrance to Westcott Bay. Howard could hear her jet ski long after she'd disappeared into the darkness beyond.

Howard almost didn't want to ask why his son had come back in completely different clothes than he'd left in. The kid was famished and ate a late dinner, the remnants of sandwiches Karen had made. He ate three of them and downed it all with several glasses of milk before collapsing on his fold-down dinette bed and falling into a sleep so deep, he didn't stir even when his phone beeped on receiving a text message.

Meagan grabbed it and checked for him before Howard or Karen could scold her for invading her brother's privacy. "Thanks again and have a good night's sleep," she read from the screen. "It's from Sidney. And it's not even good blackmail material." Disgusted, she tossed the phone back and crawled into her own bed.

Howard and Karen pulled up deck chairs and watched the night sky together. The night was uneventful except hourly when Howard got up to look back at the boom. In fact, with the gentle lapping of water against the ship, it was quite peaceful. Looking upwards, it was almost like falling into the stars, the vastness of it leaving him a bit lightheaded. He started searching for constellations he knew, but could only find the big dipper. Just as he thought he'd found Orion's Belt, a shooting star streaked through the blackness, so quick it could easily have been a trick of the eye.

"Did you see that?"

"See what?" Karen asked.

"There was a shooting star. Look! Another one."

She saw that time. He could tell from the way she let out a soft gasp.

"And another!" she called.

They watched for several minutes as the night sky filled with shooting stars, meteors burning up as they entered Earth's atmosphere. They flashed for a brief second and left a faint trail of light in their wake.

"It's August, isn't it?" Karen mused.

"Yeah?"

"They're the Perseid meteor showers," she said with determination. "They pass through the Earth's orbit once a year. And here we are, at just the right place to enjoy them."

Howard leaned back in his chair and watched as the meteor shower continued. It was nice to think that for once today he was in the right place at the right time. Maybe things would be smooth sailing from here on.

Chapter 12

‒‒‒‒‒‒‒‒ ⌒⊗⊗⊗⌒ ‒‒‒‒‒‒‒‒

D ay Two of what the press was calling the Haro Strait Crisis—some of the cuter ones dubbed it "dire straits in Haro Strait"—dawned early. Kirby woke at 5:30 to a call from Ms. Kurosawa, who told him Cooper Andrews, the bigtime national reporter for CCN, would be arriving at Friday Harbor by plane at 7:00. That gave Kirby just enough time to shower, dress, and check in with folks.

During the check-in process Kirby got involved in an energetic online debate about whether dispersants should be used on the slick. He said he'd researched their use in Prince William Sound and his resounding conclusion was that they did more harm than good. Kirby reiterated some of the same scientific arguments he'd stated the day before in his discussions on the subject with Jack and Shannon.

During the dispersant discussion, Kirby received positive feedback from administrators and scientists at the National Marine Fisheries Service. They'd heard reports of the drama with the oil and how Kirby's scheme using the naval sonar tapes had turned back the orcas. Kirby couldn't help but think it might help his grant-writing with them and other funders in the future.

Shannon was busy coordinating with SOSA, scheduling volunteer vessels and helping direct them to where they needed to go. Jack was helping from the beach. Howard Strander reported all was fine with the booms, though he did voice concern about whether the anchors alone would be enough to hold the boom in place on the ebb tide, which would be at maximum current at 10:30 a.m.

"If your son's up to it, have him and Sidney do a couple runs back and forth checking the boom," Kirby suggested as he struggled with a tie before throwing it aside as a ridiculous idea. His years as a field scientist had left him largely a stranger to formal attire.

Ms. Kurosawa was waiting for Kirby at the Friday Harbor Airport. Her own Channel Five plane was parked near the hangars. Kirby dreaded facing her overly enthusiastic handshake again, but before that happened; an unmarked plane came in from the west over Dallas Mountain, unexpectedly heading east toward the airport. The plane landed, the stairway was unfolded, and a face Kirby had often seen on the national news station appeared.

"Michele," Cooper Andrews said, greeting Ms. Kurosawa first. He didn't seem put-off by her handshake, giving her a wide smile in return. "So, what have you got for me?" He turned to Kirby. "You're the whale expert, right?" He offered his hand.

"This is Kirby Jackson, with the Whale Research Institute." Ms. Kurosawa explained. "He's been the leader calling for and positioning a boom to protect an environmentally sensitive area and working to keep the orcas separated from the oil."

"Thanks for coming out here," Kirby said, taking Mr. Andrews's hand. "We hope to get the message out there that these sorts of incidents happen and can have a disastrous effect on the environment." He pointed to the plane behind them. "If you don't mind my asking, you folks came in from an unexpected direction. Seattle is southeast of here; your plane came from the west."

"Got a few flyover shots of the wreck up north first," Mr. Andrews's cameraman answered. He'd had an entire crew with him, with equipment much more sophisticated than Ms. Kurosawa's.

"How's it looking up there?" Kirby asked.

"The oil's actually pretty hard to see," the cameraman went on, "except where the light hits in the direction of the sun." He seemed almost disappointed it wasn't more dramatic.

Kirby could give them all the dramatic footage they wanted. He cocked his head for them to follow him. "I suggest we drive over to Roche Harbor and check out the marine mammal and bird rescue operation before going to my place to get out on the water."

They piled into the Channel Five News van, which shuttled them across the island. On the way, Kirby briefly spelled out the history of Roche Harbor for Andrews's benefit. "This territory was in dispute between the U.S. and Great Britain in the day. Have you ever heard of the Pig War?"

"Can't say I have," Andrews said with a bemused smile.

"In 1859, an American farmer shot and killed a free-roaming pig that had wandered onto his property. The pig belonged to his neighbor, who worked for the British Hudson Bay Company. The farmer offered to pay the man for the pig, but his neighbor wanted a higher price. The British authorities threatened to have the farmer arrested, and the American government countered with military escalation. Even President Buchanan got involved. We were practically on the eve of the Civil War, so Buchanan didn't want to go to war with the British Empire over a pig. He calmed things down, and now it's more like a humorous footnote in our history."

Andrews nodded, indicating understanding.

"Roche Harbor, where we're headed, later became a limestone mining area. The big hotel there was originally built to house mining staff. Now it's a destination for vacationers and pleasure crafts."

"It certainly is a beautiful area," Andrews said.

"We'd like to keep it that way," Kirby replied.

They reached Roche Harbor, where the volunteers were out in full force even though it was barely 7:30 a.m. Kirby took the cameraman through the tent, where men and women in heavy rubber gloves had begun cleaning the first of the animals using warm water and a mild detergent. The cameraman took several shots of the birds as volunteers ran gloved fingers through sticky feathers. Except for sloshing water in the plastic tubs and the occasional frantic flap of wings, it was the eerily silent for a place with so many animals under its roof.

"Can I help with the seals?"

The cameraman swung around to catch a young girl trying to get one of the volunteers' attentions. She had brown hair and wore a blue and green windbreaker. Kirby knew she didn't belong here. Kirby got her attention.

"Sorry, miss, but only trained volunteers can touch the animals."

The young girl pouted. "That's not fair. My brother got to handle a bird yesterday, and I'm the one studying marine animals."

"Your brother, eh?" Kirby stroked his chin. "Are you Jason's sister, by chance?" He remembered the gangly kid from yesterday and admitted there was a certain family resemblance between them.

"I'm Meagan Strander. Mom and I hitched a ride up with one of those boom guys to get a shower," she said.

"Right, the Stranders. Yesterday you helped with the speakers and now your dad's tending the booms, isn't he?"

"You're the guy from the radio," she said. "Kirby Jackson, right? I read the book about you. What was it? *Whale Wars*."

Kirby lifted his eyebrows in surprise. "It's called *War of the Whales*."

"Yeah, the one about the effects of military sonar on whales and a lot about your life with whales." She walked over and plopped herself onto a stool right next to him, heedless of the cameras, though the cameraman seemed to be eating it up. "We came all the way out here to see whales, and it turns out we've been chasing them off." She flipped her hair over one shoulder. "For their own good, of course. I read in your book that breathing concentrated oil fumes near the surface can cause disorientation and even suffocation in whales and porpoises, so I guess I'd rather keep them away from here, even if it means I don't get to see as many."

Kirby chuckled and resisted the urge to ruffle the kid's hair. "Hey, after this, I'm taking my friends here"—he pointed to Mr. Andrews and his crew—"out on the water to see the whales. I don't suppose you'd like to come along?"

Meagan's jaw dropped and her eyes went as wide as saucers. "I...I..." She jumped up from her seat. "I'll go ask my mom!"

She was off in a flash, leaving Kirby and the news crew chuckling.

"Looks like you got yourself a protégé," Andrews laughed.

By the time the cameraman had filmed enough footage of the animals and clean-up operations, Meagan returned with a distinct bounce in her step. They all hopped into the Channel Five News van again and took off with one minor in tow. Kirby sat shotgun, giving directions to his home and office on the western shore and pointing out spots of interest as they went: the sculpture park, the American and British history sites, the oyster-filled Wescott Bay, which, he pointed out, they had so far protected from oil.

Upon getting out of the van, Kirby invited them into his office. On the way in, he noticed the cameraman getting shots of his yard littered with coils of rope, anchors, buoys, oars, dead outboard motors, and boats of various sizes and shapes that had seen better days. Oh well, *c'est la vie.* Too late to tidy things up now.

Inside was not much better. Books, magazines, papers, CDs, tapes, and VHF cassettes along with a half dozen computers and fax machines were scattered about on desks, shelves, and the floor. Wall space was completely occupied with pictures of orcas with names and numbers listed on each along with family and pod genealogy charts. He explained a little about the Center for Whale Research's Whale ID project he'd spent the last thirty years working on. Andrews and his crew listened in quiet interest, but it was Meagan who clung to his every word and often interrupted to ask questions.

"How'd you get started studying whales?" she asked.

"Well…I grew up in Miami. My father was a fisherman, so I was out on the boats a lot. I used to watch the dolphins for hours whenever they came around to eat the fish my father would throw back for them. They were almost humanlike in their intelligence. Soon I learned to tell them apart, which group individual animals belonged to. Then I went to school at UC Davis, and it was there that I saw my first orca."

He described the flashback of his first gray encounter, the roiling of the water as they surrounded the boat. He remembered leaning over the side to see one big eye, black and full of serene, ancient wisdom staring back at him.

"I fell in love with them," he said, "and suddenly I knew what I was put on this Earth to do."

Meagan's eyes were wide and glistening as she listened.

"I graduated UC Davis with a bachelor's in zoology, then I went to graduate school at UC Santa Cruz, where I got my masters in marine mammal biology. It was a lot of hard work and studying." He gave her a meaningful look. "So you'd better keep up yours grades, missy."

She gave him a mock salute.

The radio at his belt crackled and he answered.

"Kirby," Jack's enthusiastic voice said, "I'm calling to tell you it looks like the J's may be on roughly the same schedule as yesterday. They're already just east of Eagle Point and heading your way steadily. Should be a good opportunity in case you're interested in putting on a show for your new friends."

"Ah, well" Kirby stammered, looking and sounding self-conscious, almost embarrassed at Jack's kidding.

"We sure look forward to seeing you on the national news," Jack said, laughing before cutting out.

"Let's go find some whales," Kirby announced. "They're not too far away."

***

Meagan could barely contain herself as they made their way down to the beach. She didn't even mind having to wear another stupid-looking life jacket before boarding Mr. Jackson's inflatable orange pontoon boat. The news people—she was pretty sure she'd seen the one guy on television before, standing in strong wind during a storm—took seats near the bow while she took a seat next to where Mr. Jackson stood at the steering console.

"It's about a fifteen-minute ride," Kirby said, raising his voice to be heard over the motor.

Meagan gave him her best are-you-kidding-me look. "I flew over a thousand miles to see some darn whales," she said and was glad her mother wasn't there to yell at her to watch her language. "Fifteen more minutes isn't anything."

They took off at a good clip. The pontoon boat was much lower to the water than the *Serendipity*, and sea spray came over the gunnels. Meagan leaned over slightly and let her hand slide through the cold water, watching it slip through her fingers.

"Careful," Mr. Jackson said. "You don't want to fall in now."

"I won't, Mr. Jackson."

"Kirby," he said. "Please, call me Kirby."

As they headed farther from land, Kirby checked his GPS every so often. Meagan was torn between looking over her shoulder for large shapes to appear underwater and watching bow-ward for the telltale dorsal fins to break through the water.

In the end, it was the cameraman who alerted them, standing abruptly and pointing out into the water. "There!" he called. "Something just surfaced."

"Could be a seal or a dolphin," the anchorman said thoughtfully.

Kirby checked his GPS. "No, looks like those are our whales." He puttered slightly farther and then killed the engine, letting them drift on the current. "Let's wait here for them."

They didn't have long to wait. First Meagan saw the dorsal fins, unmistakable, even against the uneven waves. Then, the occasional shiny black head would come to the surface, exhaling large blasts of water and air before dipping back down. Two or three, she thought, running to the bow to get a better look. The closer they swam, the more Meagan could see, until she could make out easily a dozen orcas in total. And they were headed right for their boat.

Suddenly, one of the bigger male orcas—his dorsal fin was larger than that of the females—surged forward and burst out of the water. His great white belly flashed in the sunlight as he rolled over, smacking the water and disappearing with an incredible splash.

"That's J26," Kirby said, hands in his pockets as he came to join them at the front of the boat. "He's a real showoff, that one. The boys usually are." He pointed to a large female swimming amidst the others. "And there's J2, Granny. She recently celebrated her one hundredth birthday."

"No way!" Meagan said. She'd known orcas could live as long as, sometimes longer than, humans, but to think this whale had been around before even her grandparents were born was unreal.

A flash of umber among all the white and black caught her attention. "That small one," the commentator said, "is it sick?"

"Naw," Kirby said. "That's just how they look when they're babies. That's the newest addition to J pod," Kirby went on, "J49. We're not sure if the little guy is, well, a guy for certain yet, but we do know it's Granny's great-great-grandchild."

The orcas milled about, seemingly unperturbed by their little boat. In fact, they almost seemed to enjoy the attention, sometimes rolling over or smacking their flukes to raise a great spray of water in their wakes. One even launched herself into the air, a full-on breach, and hung there suspended for what seemed like forever before plummeting back into the water below.

Meagan could have watched them all day, but they passed on, presumably in search of salmon.

"Amazing animals," the commentator said as Kirby turned to head back towards home.

They headed up the west shore of San Juan Island towards Mosquito Pass and the boom Jason and Sidney had helped tow across and secure in place. The *Serendipity* was anchored just south of it, where Meagan's dad was in the cockpit dutifully watching the boom. Meagan waved to him from the pontoon, and he did a double-take before leaning over the railing and returning the wave.

"I think you have something that belongs to me there," her dad laughed.

"Dad, we saw orcas! They were amazing!"

"How's the boom looking?" Kirby asked, pulling up alongside the *Serendipity*.

Her dad scratched at his chin, the way he did when he'd forgotten to shave that morning. "No problems here. Ebb's about over." He squinted against the light from the sun and shielded his eyes with his hands. "Is that…is that Cooper Andrews?"

"Pleased to meet you." The commentator stood and shook hands with her dad over the railing. "You're one of the volunteers manning the boom out here?"

Her dad's face grew red. "Uh…yeah, something like that."

As Meagan climbed from the pontoon boat to the sailboat, her nimble figure ducking under the metal railing, Sidney and Jason arrived on their jet ski. "Hey, Mr. Jackson!" Sidney called, standing and offering him a wave. She was wearing the same hat she'd had on when she'd picked Jason up yesterday. Meagan supposed that if Jason was going to have a girlfriend, he could do worse than Sidney.

"You two volunteers as well?" Cooper asked, his eyes shining brightly with the prospect of adding the daring exploits of attractive young teens to his footage.

"Jason and Sidney helped set up this boom, and the one at Mitchell Harbor," Kirby said. "They towed it from here to there." He followed the path of the Mosquito Pass boom, immediately in front of them, with his finger from the opposite shore to Henry Island.

"Really?" The commentator stood and shook their hands. "Could you possibly re-enact towing on the boom? Strictly for the camera, of course."

Meagan rolled her eyes as she unbuckled her life jacket. "I'll be *below deck*," she called, "if anybody needs me." She'd never been one for keeping diaries, but she felt she needed to write down everything she'd seen today. *Wait 'til my science class hears about this*, she thought as she made her way down to the cabin.

—∞∞∞—

As they headed out from the *Serendipity*, Kirby turned to Cooper Andrews. "Say, before you leave, I just wanted to emphasize that, as bad as this spill is, compared to what we'd have if one of those thirty-odd fully laden tankers per month they're proposing to send down Haro Straits were to collide or hard ground, this spill is miniscule. There would be booms like this attempting, in most cases futilely, to block oil from reaching bays, inlets, and shorelines from Seattle to Vancouver. This place would never be the same. Never! And thankful as we are that the Keystone pipeline has been set back, there will be even more pressure to send that nasty oil through here."

Cooper thought a moment. "Remember, I spent weeks having to witness and report on the Gulf Oil Disaster, and I also remember Exxon-Valdez."

Kirby replied, "Need I say more?"

Chapter 13

It was best that Kirby, Andrews, and the cameraman had dropped Meagan off where they did, Kirby thought as they motored up the western shoreline of Henry Island towards the grounded freighter, as it was important to limit the amount of exposure she had to the unrefined oil fumes. He knew from the Exxon-Valdez experience that even short-term exposure could cause respiratory irritation.

They encountered another of the islands of kelp, sticks, and various other oil-lathered debris just off Kellett Bluff. Kirby watched the cameraman film a close-up of a dead bird amidst the oily mass. He suspected this was the sort of footage they'd wanted. Kirby could only think of the misery the unsuspecting creature had gone through. The camera crew never stopped filming until Kirby pulled away.

At Turn Point, ground zero, there was an oil film around the freighter, thick and sickly brown near the ship. However, it didn't look like much new oil was being emitted.

Farther from the ship, the oil thinned out and took on the hues of the rainbow, deceptively colorful in contrast to its potential for harm, Kirby thought. The booms were now in place surrounding the ship. A Coast Guard boat kept Kirby's vessel from getting too close, stopping him at a distance of two hundred feet with a loudspeaker. Kirby drifted among the number of pleasure boats looking on from the safety perimeter.

Another freighter had been brought in with a crane swinging between the two ships as the grounded vessel was relieved of the containers that could be reached with the makeshift unloading apparatus. The *Bel Amica*'s fuel tanks had emptied themselves.

Kirby turned back to the southeast and sped home. Arriving at the makeshift boom Oly and his Scandinavian fish-mates had set up, Kirby, Andrews, and the cameraman removed their shoes, rolled up their pants, and stepped into the knee-deep frigid water of Puget Sound. The crude oil-absorbing boom appeared to be doing the job as the various absorbent materials were now darkened and gave off a strong petroleum odor. Kirby commented, "Those fishermen are pretty resourceful. They had these manufactured and installed within five hours after we planted the seed."

The entourage scampered up the hill toward Kirby's van.

Andrews asked, "Say, Kirby, could we take a quick peek at that apparatus you used to turn the whales back yesterday?"

"Sure thing, right over here."

Kirby and his cameraman followed and examined an early mock-up of the simple device.

"That's it?" Andrews asked.

"Sure is," Kirby said. "Not much to look at, is there?"

"No, not exactly what I was expecting."

"Listen, I'll grab a recording of the Navy sonar tape and play it while we're traveling back to the airport, and you can hear a subdued version of what the whales heard. Keep in mind that water is a better transmitter of sound than air and what you hear will be a tenth or less the earsplitting effect the whales experienced under Navy Sonar exercises. I'll never forget finding the dozen dead beaked whale on the shores of the Bermuda Trench after the Navy's sonar exercises back in 2000. They must have experienced very painful deaths with their ruptured ear anatomy. I've often wondered if those whales purposefully beach themselves knowing they were defenseless and wanted to get as much of their bodies out of the water as possible so sharks couldn't eat them while alive. "

Kirby mentioned that a couple of vessels would be picking up the devices shortly to reenact yesterday's scenario, as it appeared that the orcas they just witnessed were on the same path as yesterday heading for the slick. They got to the van and headed toward the airport. After listening intently to the tape for a couple of minutes, Kirby explained in greater detail how detrimental it had been to the orcas when the Navy performed sonar tests in Haro Straits. He also shared about the death of dolphins in Puget Sound with ruptured eardrums occurring shortly after Naval sonar testing in the area. He shared that the Navy had never acknowledged that their sonar was responsible for any of those incidents.

He concluded, "But while they plead lack of conclusive evidence for their activities involvement in those cases, I find it ironic they are now applying for permits to cause harm or mortality to many thousands of marine mammals in the Atlantic with new sonar tests."

"While we're on the subject of sound, you might be interested in knowing that orcas hunt their prey by echolocation. That's bouncing sound off their target prey. They can't survive without the ability to hunt with this highly refined auditory system. The point is, if we were to have these two new proposed oil and coal trans-shipment projects going forward with an additional sixty ships a month emitting up to one hundred eighty decibels in the orcas' prime hunting grounds a couple hours a day, they might starve to death over time."

After playing the hydrophone tapes, Kirby slipped Vern Olsen's "Lolita, Come Home" into the tape deck. "Check this out. It's a local group of guys singing about the orca, Lolita, that was captured in nearby Penn cove in 1970. Ever since then she's been living in a small Miami pen." He explained to Andrews about the negative effect the captures had on the resident orca population, as many of the young, soon-to-be-fertile female orcas, including Lolita, had been taken or killed.

Andrews commented, "You folks up here are obviously passionate about your orcas."

"It's hard not to be, as these are incredible animals with very large brains," Kirby responded. "From what we can gather after watching them for thirty years, they are as smart as people, in their own way, and in the best sense more human. I mean, they treat each other better than we treat our own kind. The more we observe them, the more compelled we feel to protect them from our harmful effects. So you're right, we can't help being passionate about them."

When Kirby dropped Andrews and his crew off at the airport, he hoped the footage they'd gathered would educate a nationwide audience about the plight of orcas and the impact a large spill would predictably have on them. Andrews shook his hand and thanked him one last time before boarding the plane. As they taxied down the runway, Kirby felt someone approach from behind. He turned to see Ms. Kurosawa with a smug grin on her face.

"Thank you, Ms. Kurosawa," he said. "You really came through for us."

"Hmm," she agreed with a slight hum, folding her arms over her chest. "I know a way you can repay me. Let's say…exclusive interviews when it comes time to make a documentary."

"Documentary?" Kirby chuckled.

"Sure. *Kirby Jackson, San Juan Spill Hero*. It'll be great press."

"Exclusive, you say?" Kirby raised his eyebrow. "Well…we'll discuss that when the time comes. For right now—"

As if on cue, his radio came to life.

"Kirby."

"Shannon," he answered.

"How'd everything go with the interview?"

"Good," he answered. "We'll see what gets on television, but I think it went pretty well. The whales put on a good show for our friends. Tell the Stranders they can haul the speaker up when it appears the orcas have been turned back. I heard the worst of it's over, and we've still got one boat sending sonar blasts out. That should be enough to keep them heading away."

"Got it," Shannon said. "Oh, and we've got a commercial salmon-fishing boat coming by this evening to try to capture the debris islands that skimmers can't touch. The captain says they have hydraulics heavy-duty enough to haul an entire debris mass on board with one lift. The folks at waste removal services have agreed to help with the disposal once they get it to shore."

"Yeah, I already heard," Kirby said. "I'd been trying to think of a way to remove and dispose of those awful messes the skimmer can't handle. Then, from out of nowhere, I get this call from Joe, an old acquaintance of mine, asking if he could help in any way. He shared how he'd been a seiner working on the spill in Prince William Sound and had observed how the skimmers were incapacitated when they got into floating debris mixed with the oil and he'd been thinking about how that debris could be picked up ever since. So, long story short, he jury-rigged a giant dip net that he thought would capture the debris and, aided by his powerful hydraulics, could be pulled aboard. He explained how this would also prevent those oil-soaked debris islands from hitting the beach and fouling it, let alone saving the untold man hours to clean up those tangled messes once on a beach. Irony of ironies, Joe shared that he saw his contribution in this enterprise as karma because his boat was the one that participated in the Penn Cove whale captures back in 1970 when his dad owned it. "

There was a pause and Shannon came back, "Amazing. I guess what comes around goes around."

"Yeah, back then his dad and others saw killer whales as their competitors for Chinook. Commercial and sport fishers even shot at them. Even the Navy used them for target practice during the war. Now, of course, most fishermen have done a one-eighty and wouldn't dream of harming them."

"Amazing," Shannon repeated. "Thanks for sharing that, Kirby."

"So many people turning out to help," he mused. "We need to find a way to thank them all, don't you think?"

"Well…" Shannon began, as if she'd been waiting for the right segue way. "I just got off the phone with Vern Olsen—you know, the guy with the Shifty Sailors. He and his band were already scheduled to put on a concert at Roche Harbor. Given the events of the last couple days, they've planned to morph it into a sort of fundraiser and thank you party for all the volunteers."

"Vern doesn't miss much, does he?" Kirby said. "If you give Vern the go-ahead, I'll see about getting the word out. I know there are several folks I'd like to invite personally."

As Shannon made the appropriate plans, Kirby called the Stranders' vessel.

"Say, Howard," Kirby said. "What are your plans for Thursday after the ungrounding attempt? I hear tell Vern Olsen would very much like to see your family again at the Shifty Sailors' Roche concert."

SPILL

Howard said yes to Kirby, but thought, *Will they thank me or roast me?*

With all the excitement over the last two days, Howard had completely forgotten his "back problems." But now that things had calmed down—the oil was evaporating, the debris islands were being wrangled in, and the animals were in the process of being cleaned—the thought came back. *It's my fault all this happened.* The bottle of OxyContin called to him from the salon. He downed a couple pills and chased it down with water from the boat faucet before considering bottled water would have been better. For several moments, he watched himself in the small mirror above the sink. His skin was sun-kissed from hours on deck, manning the boom and the underwater speaker, but the North Dakota businessman still stared back at him.

Ironically, now Kirby had radioed to invite him to some big concert in Roche Harbor, like he was a VIP, a guest of honor. A hero.

I'm no hero, he thought as he looked into the reflection. *I'm a villain.*

"Dad!"

He heard Meagan's frantic cry. Abandoning his self-pity, he bolted above deck to find her leaning halfway over the railing, gesturing wildly towards a clump of oil drifting along the boom towards them. As he came up behind her to see what she was pointing at and yanked her back from leaning too far over the railing, he thought he saw some movement in the tangled mess of kelp and driftwood.

"There's an otter stuck in there," Meagan said. "We've got to save it."

"Honey," Howard called and Karen came quickly.

"What? What is it? I heard Meagan yelling and—" She put a hand to her heart in relief upon seeing nobody had gone overboard. "You scared me near to death."

Howard pointed out the trapped otter. "I'm going to pull the boat around," he said. "Think you can grab it with the salmon dip net?"

Karen eyed the moving mass skeptically. "Do we have one big enough?"

Karen found the dip net in one of the storage areas. Howard maneuvered the *Serendipity* into position, and Karen leaned over the bow with the net. As the boat came alongside the boom, she made a grab for the struggling animal. The net caught hold of it, but when she tried to yank it back, it caught. She called to Howard for assistance.

"Here, honey, take the controls." Howard shifted into neutral and ran to the bow. "If we need to get closer, just let up on the throttle and the current will take us closer to the poor thing. Once I've got the otter, shift into reverse to get us back away from the boom. Think you can do that?"

Karen nodded. "Good thing I can drive a stick shift," she laughed, but her face was pale. She took her position at the helm and brought them forward gently.

Howard gripped the net and reached out as far as he could. "I think I've got it," he called triumphantly. The tiny wriggling mass of matted fur and oil lifted from the debris island with a plop. Carefully, he began to pull it toward him. "Okay, back up now," he said.

Karen made a weak effort at pulling away. She was trigger-shy.

"Gun it a little, hon."

The motor revved and the sailboat lurched backwards. Before Howard could yell to throttle down or had the presence of mind to let go of the net, which had caught firmly on a large stick, he was pulled off the smooth, polished fiberglass deck and plunged deep into the icy cold waters of Puget Sound. The strong flood current swept him under the floating matt of oil-soaked debris.

Chapter 14

Howard heard no sound, could discern no up or down. He had never been an especially strong swimmer, but this was like floundering through cold molasses, molasses that sapped the breath from his body. He attempted to kick with his legs and flail with his arms, but they barely moved as they met unrelenting resistance from the tangle of kelp, sticks, and other debris the swirling currents had brought together against the boom. He couldn't tell if he was moving towards the surface, or whether he was even moving at all.

His mouth opened in a silent scream, and his mouth was filled with tarry, oily saltwater.

I'm going to die, he thought as everything within him and around him became numb, wrapped in an immense cocoon of nothingness. *I still have so much to do, to make up for. Meagan, Jason, Karen…I'm so sorry.*

Karen screamed. She had released the throttle, but the boat continued to drift backward, leaving Howard behind. All she could see was a black hand poking up through the oily mass.

"Oh my God! Howard!" She abandoned the controls and ran to the spot where her husband had fallen overboard. The deck was slippery, and she might have gone in herself had Meagan not cried out just then, grabbing her around her waist, rooting her to the spot.

"Mom, careful, or you'll fall in too," her daughter said.

Karen forced herself to stop. Meagan was right. She couldn't afford to panic. Howard couldn't afford for her to panic.

"Honey," she said in a shaking voice, turning and grasping Meagan's shoulders, "I need you to find something for your father to grab onto."

Meagan nodded. Even though she looked like she wanted to cry, recognizing the demanding situation, she remained focused.

"There's a life ring in the cockpit," Karen screamed. "Go, hurry."

As Meagan hurried off to get the life ring, Karen made her way more carefully to the forward edge of the bow railing. The current carried the boat up next to the oily mass of debris. Gripping the railing tightly, she leaned over as far as she dared. "Howard!" His hand had disappeared. She didn't even know where to find him now. "Howard, can you hear me?"

There was no reply.

The shrill whine of a motor drew her attention. She looked up to see Sidney on her jet ski, Jason seated behind her. They pulled up alongside the *Serendipity.* "We heard a scream," Jason said. "What's wrong, Mom?"

"It's your father!" The calmness she'd been trying to maintain broke, and her voice cracked into a sob. "He's fallen in. He's under the oil."

All the color left Jason's face. "Sidney," he said, "bring me around next to the boom. I'll get Dad out."

"Be careful," Karen warned. Her heart beat rapidly in the hollow of her throat at the thought of her son going in as well.

Sidney circled as close to the boom as she could, sidling up with a cold-blooded expertise that Karen envied. Jason slid off the craft and straddled the boom.

"Oh, oh, be careful." Words fell like a meaningless mantra from Karen's lips.

Meagan reappeared at her side, breathless and carrying the life ring. She paled further when she saw Jason sitting on the boom but tossed him the ring when he held out his hands to catch it. He plunged it into the oily mass where Karen pointed, indicating where Howard's hand had disappeared.

"Howard!" Karen screamed, hoping against hope that he could hear her. "Grab hold of the ring. Grab hold. Don't let go."

"He's pulling back," Jason said, giving the ring a tug. "I think it's him." He pulled harder on the ring and Howard's arm emerged with the crook of his elbow, covered in tarry black oil, around the life ring. Jason didn't hesitate. He grabbed hold of Howard's oily wrist.

He was having a hard time of it, Karen could tell. Every time he got a decent grip, his dad's arm would slip out of his fingers, backsliding. He screwed up his face as he tried again, sinking his fingernails deep into Howard's forearm, leaving long red abrasions where they slid along his arm before sinking deep enough into his flesh to finally come up against his wrist bones, getting an adequate hold.

Howard's head poked through the oily mass, coughing and gagging uncontrollably.

"Dad!" Jason shouted. "Dad, Dad, can you breathe? Say something!"

Howard only grunted and coughed as Jason struggled to pull him toward the boom.

"Mom." It was Meagan, snapping Karen out of her stupor. "How are we going to get him into the boat?"

Karen thought momentarily about using the fold-down ladder mounted to the transom. Normally, it allowed swimmers to get back onto the boat, but she quickly assessed it probably wouldn't work to haul up a weak, lifeless, oil-slicked body.

"I'll…go get my dad," Sidney called. "He's on the right side of the boom to take him back to Roche anyway. We'll pull him aboard the low transom step."

"Right," Karen said with a firm nod. "We'll call 911."

Sidney turned her craft on a dime, flying up and over the boom in the direction of her dad's boat.

When she was gone, Karen turned back to Meagan. "Meagan, call 911. Tell them we need an ambulance at Roche Harbor as quickly as possible." She knew her daughter would act quickly, so she turned her attention back to Jason, who was so far keeping his father's head above the water. "How's he doing?"

"He's having trouble breathing!" Jason called back.

No more than a minute had gone by and Sidney reappeared, her dad in the Bayliner following her jet ski. Doug immediately understood what needed to be done, as he swung his boat around and backed the stern up next to the boom.

Jason, not letting go of Howard's wrist, maneuvered his butt onto the transom step and tugged on Howard's arm. Sidney quickly tied up her jet ski, climbed aboard, and ran to the stern, along with Doug and Tanya. Altogether, they managed to drag Howard enough to haul his convulsing, blackened, oil-slicked body up over the transom step and onto the back deck.

As he lay on the deck, Jason crouched next to him. Karen could hear Howard coughing and Jason pleading, "Say something, Dad," but she couldn't see or hear very well from a distance what was going on, and that made her nervous. "Mom," Jason called, "I...I think you need to be over here."

Her heart clenched, and suddenly she knew Jason was right and she needed to be by Howard's side.

"Hold on." Doug held up his hand to keep her from doing anything rash. "We don't want you going in as well. I'll back the boat up in as close to the boom as I can." He jogged back to his steering console, putting the engine in reverse gear to get the *Serendipity*'s bow as close to his boat's stern as possible.

Nervously, Karen edged towards the bow of the *Serendipity*, her feet unsure on the slippery deck.

"Okay." Doug was back, holding out his arms, as Sidney took the controls keeping the twin 350 engines in reverse. "Lean toward me as far as you can. I'll catch you."

"I...I don't know if I can," Karen stammered.

"We don't have much time, and Howard needs you."

That was all it took. Karen took a deep breath. Holding onto the bow rail, she swung both legs over the rail and took a step forwards, suspended over a black hole of oil. Her mind was a blind panic until she felt Doug's arms guide her the rest of the way across.

No time to congratulate Doug or herself, though. Howard's coughing and gagging brought her back to the situation at hand. She knelt by his side and took his face between her hands. His entire body was covered with oil and seaweed. He didn't seem to be able to talk or open his eyes.

"Howard, honey, can you hear me?"

Howard grunted unintelligibly, but at least he seemed to understand the question.

She swallowed hard. "Howard, honey, we're taking you up to a hospital. Just hold on."

"Mom!" It was Meagan, calling from the *Serendipity*. The space between the two ships was within jumping distance, and yet it felt like a vast chasm.

"Honey, stay there!" Karen screamed. "Don't try to jump!"

"But, Mom—"

"I got it, Mrs. Strander." Karen barely had time to recognize Sidney's voice before the girl was jumping back onto her jet ski. "I'll take care of Meagan and your boat. You just get Mr. Strander to the hospital."

Karen nodded in gratitude. She turned to tell Doug to hurry, but he was already rushing back to the controls.

"Mom!" Meagan yelled, holding her phone. "A van is waiting at Roche to rush Dad to the hospital."

"We'll have to improvise a stretcher then," Jason said. "Do you think a sleeping bag will do?"

Tanya nodded and ran back into the cabin as Doug put the boat into drive and took off at full throttle. Tanya reappeared a second later carrying the bag. She unzipped it and spread it wide open. Karen and Jason worked together to move Howard onto it as he continued to gag and cough.

Karen used a corner of the sleeping bag to wipe the oil from his eyes. "We're going to take you to the hospital," she said.

Howard again only grunted. It sounded like he was trying to say something.

"Water?" Karen asked, and he nodded weakly.

Tanya fetched a water bottle from the cooler on deck. Karen held Howard's head up and dribbled a little between his lips. He gagged, coughed, and spit it out.

Karen gave him a few seconds to recover before asking, "Do you want to try again?"

Howard seemed to nod affirmatively. Karen trickled some more water into his mouth. This time, instead of spitting it out, he swallowed, as a little escaped the side of his mouth. She repeated the procedure, and each time Howard seemed a little more in control.

He once tried to open his eyes but quickly closed them again.

Doug's intimate familiarity with Mosquito Pass allowed him to shorten the travel time to Roche by cutting corners inside the navigation buoys that marked shoals and rocks exposed at a lower tide. Doug had covered the three miles up the pass in six minutes. He ignored the signs imploring boaters to slow down and "leave no wake" as they approached the marina. As they came up to the dock, Jason jumped over the transom step onto the dock in one swift move and tied the boat's stern to the dock quickly.

With each of the four of them lifting a corner of the makeshift stretcher, they moved Howard off the boat and up the dock to the van, waiting with open back doors. The driver and his assistant helped lift Howard aboard and covered him with blankets. Karen climbed in, assuring them she was his wife, and sat holding his hand as one of the EMTs propped his head up with a pillow. The back doors closed and they sped off toward the Friday Harbor hospital.

Chapter 15

Karen steadied Howard's body as the van sped around the sharp turns of the winding country road. She talked to him, trying to get him to stay with her as she explained what was happening. He made grunting noises every so often, but mostly he coughed and choked.

"The doctor will know what to do. We should be there soon, honey. You're going to be okay. Don't try to talk."

Upon arriving, the EMTs put him on a gurney and then hurried him into the emergency exam room. Karen was informed it was a restricted area, so she was left wringing her hands in the waiting room.

Howard couldn't see or speak, but he could hear. Everything sounded like it was muffled through seven layers of cotton, but it was still something, some way of knowing what was going on around him.

"Mr. Strander," a voice said, and Howard didn't know who it was. It didn't sound like Karen. She wouldn't call him "Mr. Strander." "I'm Doctor Singh. Do you know where you are?"

Howard couldn't answer.

"You're at the Peace Island Medical Center's Emergency Room. You've had an accident. I'm just going to check your vitals here. Try not to move."

Howard felt fingers poking and prodding him, feeling his pulse, taking his temperature, measuring his blood pressure. A couple of latex-gloved fingers opened his mouth, and he felt the doctor lean over to inspect his throat.

"Looks like you swallowed and probably inhaled some oil, my friend," Dr. Singh said. "We're going to have to do a stomach lavage and try to get as much out as possible. But first I'm going to flush your eyes and then get some protecting ointment on them."

Howard was barely able to mumble, "O…o…okay."

His eyelids were pried open by a nurse. The blurry shapes of white-coat-clad people moved back and forth in his swimming vision as the doctor flushed and treated his eyes. His vision cleared, but he couldn't tell if the wetness in his eyes was from the ointment or his own tears.

He could now see the doctor more clearly. Singh wore a surgical mask, but he had kind eyes, and that reassured Howard as he said, "Okay, Mr. Strander, here comes the uncomfortable part: the stomach tube. We'll put a little local anesthetic spray where it slides through your nose and over your epiglottis, but you'll still want to gag. That's normal. Sorry to have to put you through this, but it's necessary, I assure you."

Howard couldn't help gagging and coughing as the doctor slid the tube slowly into place.

Dr. Singh kept talking him through it. "We're going to pump your stomach until the return fluid is free of oil, then we'll coat your stomach and intestines to try and protect them from any residue."

The process was unpleasant. A "mild cleansing fluid"—it didn't feel so mild to Howard, but that's what the doctor kept calling it—was pumped in and back out. This was repeated three times. Next the protective coating medicine was pumped into his stomach, and then, thankfully, it was done. The tube came out and Howard hacked and coughed as it was pulled free.

"We're not going to suppress that cough for now," Dr. Singh said as a nurse handed him a clipboard. "You need that reflex to help prevent an aspiration pneumonia. What I'm going to do now is put some antibiotics into your IV, along with some gentle sedatives so you can relax a little. But first, let's get you cleaned up a bit."

The doctor left the dirty work to the nurse as he left the room to update Karen on Howard's condition.

Karen's phone rang. It was Meagan.

"Mom, where are you? How's Dad?"

Karen updated her on all that had happened since they'd abruptly left in their haste to get Howard to the hospital. "The doctors have administered emergency treatment and are watching him real close. I think he's expected to recover. But he's not out of the woods yet."

"Do you want me to come to the hospital?" Meagan asked. "Kirby said we don't need to tow the boom anymore, as the tide has let up. Sidney and I are free to leave, and I'd really like to be there. Sidney can give me a ride to Roche after we anchor the *Serendipity*."

"Dad's mumbled your name like he was asking about you. You helped save his life back there, throwing the life ring to Jason so quickly and accurately." Karen felt tears well in her eyes. "We're so proud of you."

"I just did what I had to do."

"I know. You...and Jason...and Sidney...you were all great." She dabbed at her eyes with a bit of wadded-up tissue. The clicking of shoes on the tile floor told her she needed to end this call. "I need to go, honey. The doctor's here again."

Dr. Singh smiled, which meant good news. Karen let out a long, slow breath before standing to greet him. "Mrs. Strander," he said, "we've moved your husband to recovery. The biggest threat now is pneumonia, and we'll be taking x-rays of his lungs every twelve hours to monitor that. He ate a little. Just Jell-O for now, but so far he's been able to keep it down, which is good. With a little luck he should be able to go home in a day or two."

"That's great news."

"Mind you, he's not completely in the safe yet," Dr. Singh went on. "We don't deal with a lot of oil-spattered pulmonary tissue, so we're just going off what we see now."

Karen clenched her hand around the wadded tissue and took a deep breath before asking, "Do you expect any long-term problems?"

Dr. Singh paused, but it was a thoughtful pause, not as if he were merely buying time. "Well, he both inhaled and swallowed a lot of oil. Refined oil doesn't have much acute toxicity, but this is bunker oil. I'm not certain how toxic this type of oil is, but after events like these…Exxon-Valdez, Deepwater… the primary concern for human health are certain chemical compounds found in barely-refined bunker oil, called polycyclic aromatic hydrocarbons, some of which have been found to be carcinogenic."

Karen put a hand over her mouth to stifle her gasp.

"Your husband's exposure time was relatively short and thankfully not in an aerosol form," Dr. Singh continued. "So as far as the long-term effects of short-term exposure…" He gave a helpless shrug. "We'll just have to wait and see."

Karen nodded and wondered if the knot in her stomach would ever unclench.

"Sorry I couldn't give you a more definite answer."

"No, thank you, doctor," she said, regaining her composure. "I appreciate you being upfront with me about this."

He gave an apologetic smile before leaving to recheck Howard.

Karen slumped into her chair and waited for her heartbeat to return to normal. After this was all said and done, she wondered, how many more families would be in a position similar to hers due to overexposure to toxic hydrocarbons? Waiting out the rest of their days to see if their loved ones had suffered debilitating health problems because of exposure to these chemicals? And what if Howard did develop cancer—in his lungs or throat or stomach? Would the company do its part? She laughed mirthlessly at that. No, probably not. They'd deny all responsibility, even to Howard, who had worked so hard in their industry all these years.

She was still sitting there, somewhere between numb and frantic, when the automatic doors slid back and the squeak of tennis shoes on the tile floor drew her back to the present. Meagan flung herself into her mother's arms

Sidney and Doug weren't far behind. Sidney, dressed in a gray hoodie, stepped forward. "I'm so sorry, Mrs. Strander," she said.

"Doug," Karen said, looking up to see the man's sympathetic expression, "you should be very proud of your daughter. She took control of the situation, and it's because of her and Jason and you that we were able to get Howard out of the water and to the hospital so quickly." She wiped her eyes with the back of her hand and stood, taking Sidney's hands in her own. "Thank you, so much."

Sidney blushed and Doug smiled.

"Are we allowed to see him now?" Meagan spoke up.

Karen nodded.

They found him resting in recovery, but when the door opened, he immediately struggled to prop himself up and feebly tried to hold out his arms. At the sight of her father dressed in a hospital gown, his skin pale and his hair a mess, Meagan ran into his embrace and hugged him. Karen felt herself choking up again.

"How are you feeling, Dad?" Meagan asked, face buried in Howard's shoulder.

"M...me? I'm g...great. N...never been b...betta'." Howard's voice was hoarse, and as he weakly chuckled, he began to cough.

Meagan stood back and gave her father a few hearty, open-palmed slaps to the back until the fit had calmed down.

"I thought I'd never see you again," Meagan said, fresh tears in her eyes. "It's all my fault. If I hadn't told you to get that otter—"

"Honey, honey, no." Howard grasped Meagan's hand. "*None* of this is your fault. Do you understand? Sometimes things happen...accidents. That's all. Accidents happen. You can't control them. That's why they're called accidents." He grew silent for a moment, and Karen wondered what went on in his head as he stared off at some distant point.

Everyone stuck around for about an hour before Doug finally suggested it was time to let Howard get some rest.

"Kirby's going to take me out to see whales again," Meagan announced.

"And Sidney and I are going to watch the ungrounding," Jason said. "We'll have front row seats at Turn Point."

Howard raised his eyebrows.

"It'll be perfectly safe, Mr. Strander," Sidney said. "We're not even going to be that close to the boat, really. We'll have a good view from the elevated rock above the lighthouse." She pointed to the TV screen mounted on the opposite wall. "They'll be broadcasting it. You can watch from your room, if you want."

Very slowly he said, "Okay, just be careful."

With a final round of hugs, Doug ushered everyone out. Karen was about to follow—the last twenty-four hours were beginning to catch up with her, along with all the sweat and grime that came from not having showered—but Howard grabbed hold of her hand and held her back.

"Karen." His voice was still scratchy as he spoke in a low, contemplative tone. "I've been thinking. It's going to be hard for me to return to my work after all this."

Karen smiled sympathetically. "Honey, maybe it's time to make some changes."

"But the kids...and Jason's going to college soon..."

Karen ran a hand through his hair. It was messy and still a little slick. "We'll work something out. I know your job has been making you unhappy for years. It's the reason you..." She trailed off. They'd never discussed the OxyContin. "You always take on too much blame," she began again. "It's true what you said to Meagan, you know."

He looked at her, not quite comprehending.

"You don't have any control over accidents. I know you think this whole... situation is your fault, but it's not. It was an accident, honey. I think everyone understands that."

Howard shook his head. "Everyone knows I'm responsible. I ruined everything."

"No, no." She made soft shushing noises, like she'd done to the children when they'd had to stay home from school with the flu. "You need to stop being so hard on yourself. Imagine what the kids would do if anything happened to you. Imagine what *I* would do if anything happened to you." She leaned in and planted a gentle kiss against his forehead. "Please don't ever scare me like that again. My heart couldn't take it."

Chapter 16

J ason and Sidney spent the whole van ride back to the harbor googily-eyeing
each other, making Meagan more than ready to get out by the time they
arrived. The next morning, with some of her worries about her father allayed,
Meagan was looking forward to getting back out on the water again.

After a good sleep and a hearty breakfast, Meagan left the inn and searched
the crowd of volunteers for Kirby. He was easy to spot in his khakis and Hawaiian
shirt.

"Kirby!" She waved and bounded over to him. "Sorry we're up so late."

"No problem," he said, waving to some nearby volunteers to indicate he was
taking a break. "I'm surprised you made it with all you've been through."

Sidney and Jason were close behind.

"Is there much oil around today?" Sidney asked.

"There's a fairly persistent sheen." Kirby shielded his eyes and looked out
across the harbor. "It's not thick, but it's pretty widespread. It's probably just
going to hang around for a while until it all evaporates or gets absorbed by a
beach or a bird...whichever it hits first."

"Speaking of birds," Jason cut in, "how is the bird-cleaning going?"

"Mixed, as you might expect. It mostly depends on how badly they were
oiled. Of the two hundred or so brought in, something under half will probably
make it."

Meagan felt like she might cry hearing that, but she appreciated Kirby's directness. Plenty of people tried to sugarcoat bad news when dealing with young people.

He seemed to know her thoughts, because he clapped her on the back and said, "Cheer up, kiddo. There are plenty more animals around here that could use our help." He cocked his head towards the dock. "I'm going to be making the rounds, checking up on some beaches and the freighter. You want to come along?"

"My mom totally trusts you and said I can go with you anytime you offer. Will there be whales?"

"I can't guarantee." He scratched at his beard. "'Course, there's work to do, too. We'll wind up at the grounded freighter to watch her liberation, if all goes well," he said with up raised eyebrows. "I heard rumors there could possibly be some hurdles with the ungrounding."

"What sort of hurdles?" Meagan asked.

"Nothing you need to worry about. They can't access the ship's manifesto because the computers went down when the electrical system was damaged at the grounding and..." He stopped talking to look down at her. "Aw, no need to bore you with the details."

"It won't be dangerous to be there to watch, will it?" Sidney asked. "Jason and I were going to take the Jet Ski to Prevost and then hike over to watch the ungrounding from above Turn Point."

"You should be safe. Just don't get too close to the ship."

"We won't," she promised, rocking back and forth on her feet. "We're going to watch from the bluff overlooking the freighter. I checked with the Coast Guard to make sure it was okay to motor to Prevost, and they said that would be fine."

Meagan didn't really see the appeal. Sure, watching the ungrounding of the big ship from the rock overlook would be exciting, but for her money, she'd rather be on the water watching. If Sidney and Jason wanted to hold hands and kiss or whatever, she was glad to not be a part of it. She made a face at Kirby as they walked towards the dock, indicating her distaste for the whole teenager thing. He laughed.

—❦❦❦—

There was a certain irony in seeing the seventy-year-old Kirby attempting to assist twelve-year-old Meagan as she virtually flew over the gunnel boarding his orange-red inflatable pontoon craft. They motored out of the marina and through the northern portal to Mosquito Pass, past Pearl Island, and into Speiden Pass. Kirby turned to the northwest toward the wreckage.

Pointing to the west, Meagan named off the geography she remembered from the *Serendipity*'s maps. "Sidney Island, Gooch Island, Rum Island…which means that's…um, Tom Point." She pointed out the narrow gap of water separating Tom Point from Turn Point.

"Pretty good," Kirby said from the helm. "We'll make a cartographer of you yet."

It was another bright, sunny day in the San Juans, and Meagan was excited to be on the water again.

Approaching the freighter, they could see the Coast Guard had their safety zone in place. Kirby idled the pontoon boat well short of the ship, about a mile from the actual wreckage.

Dozens, perhaps a hundred, private and commercial boats were out today to watch from beyond the safety zone.

"Listen, Meagan," Kirby said in a loud voice over the engine noise, "what do you say we motor on down to some of those islands you mentioned? It will probably be close to an hour before they attempt the ungrounding. I'm curious how much the oil affected that area."

"Of course I'm up for it," Meagan shouted.

Kirby immediately turned and brought their boat up on a plane heading for Sidney Island. On arrival, Kirby commented that the high tide would allow them to get in close to the beach after passing the shallows near the spit. The previous day's high had left a string of eel grass and pop weed. From a hundred feet away, it was easy to see the seaweed was covered in oil, as were the rocks and sand.

"Looks like the slick was pretty thick when it came through here on that first flood," Kirby said.

"That's not a nice way to treat Sidney's namesake island," Meagan quipped.

"I agree. Now let's cross over to Mandarte. It's that island just over there to the northeast. It's a sea bird reserve, off limits to visitors. It has nesting colonies of seagulls, guillemots, and tufted puffins."

Meagan turned from viewing the surroundings to Kirby and asked, "Kirby, before we go over there, there's one thing I need to get clear about. When I went to the whale museum and asked the nice lady why the orca population numbers were declining, she wasn't sure why but said that it was complicated. So…"

"Let me try to explain. The biggest factor in their decline is a deficit of Chinook salmon in their diet."

"Why don't they have enough?"

"Like the lady at the whale museum indicated, it's complicated or, should I say, multifaceted. Briefly, dams, overharvest, harmful development, and poor farming and forestry practices are the biggies."

"So what can we do?"

"Work on all of those. But if I could have one wish fulfilled to help, I'd remove the four lower Snake River dams to get closer to the four million Chinook needed across the resident orcas' range, roughly southeast Alaska to San Francisco. There is an undeniable correlation between the abundance of Chinook salmon and the resident orcas' population numbers, and removal of those particular dams would do more to open new prime Chinook spawning grounds, enhance smolt outmigration and spawners' return journeys than any other single restoration effort. Those four dams produce relatively small amounts of electricity, aren't as favored over and above trains for transport of grain anymore, and their removal would enhance recreational opportunities. According to the latest economic analysis their removal would create a net benefit."

"Thanks, Kirby. That helps a lot. How do you know all that?"

"I study and do research. I have to. Who else is going to do it? Not the orcas. And they don't have lobbyists to look out for them."

"Thanks, Kirby. Oh, is that a dead bird?" she asked, looking over the side and pointing.

"Yes, I was hoping you wouldn't see it. It's a pigeon guillemot. They suffered greatly in the Exxon spill. The adults eat invertebrates from shallow waters, and they are obviously very vulnerable to the oil that infiltrates the invertebrates' sandy, muddy home sites. The Prince William Sound's chicks were small and had poor survival rates. Okay, we've seen enough of that. It's time to go up to the grounded freighter and see if they're progressing."

Approaching the grounded freighter, they observed two large fireboats standing by. Megan could make out the words "San Juan Island Fire & Rescue" painted along their sides. She'd never seen a fireboat before and wondered if their presence had anything to do with the "trouble" Kirby had mentioned earlier.

"A safety precaution," he said when she asked. "I don't think it's anything to worry about, but it's rumored there might be fireworks aboard from China. With anything that potentially flammable onboard, of course they're going to have firefighting equipment on hand."

"Yeah, I guess that wouldn't be too good." Meagan shrugged and lifted her binoculars again. "It would make for an awesome scene though."

"I guess it would," Kirby said as he frowned. "They've been chipping away at the rock on the port side. From what I've been told, during the grounding, the vessel slid along that rock, splitting open the fuel tanks. When it came to a stop, the ship settled onto the rock, which penetrated deeper into the hull as the tide went out. To get the boat off, they had to remove most of the rock impaling the hull. Divers have been strategically placing small charges into the rock to gradually crumble it. Hopefully they've gotten to where she can come off. They also brought small freighter with a large crane to remove some of the containers to lighten her so she'll ride higher off the rock. Those measures, the high tide, and those super-strong tugs will hopefully be enough to get the job done."

Kirby pointed out across the water. "See those two tugs on each side of the freighter there? You can see they've taken up slack on their tethers and are beginning to put some real tension on the lines. Those are powerful tugs. Some of the new ones have ten thousand horsepower. High tide's in about a half hour, but I doubt the tide will rise more than another couple inches, so they should start towing in earnest soon. The ship will move very slowly at first. We can check to see if they're making progress by taking a sighting, lining up the stack on the freighter with the lighthouse on the point. I'll try to keep us in the same spot using my GPS. That way we'll be able to detect the slightest movement."

"The more movement the better, right?" Meagan offered.

"Well...yes, unless they end up ripping into the hull even more. Then the ship and everything in it could end up at the bottom of the channel and we'd have a different sort of mess on our hands." He gave her a reassuring smile when she threw a worried glance his way. "Let's listen to the Coasties on the radio for updates."

He flicked on the radio near the steering console.

"Coast Guard cutter San Juan to Fire Vessel Anacortes," the voice came over VHF Channel 23. "Is it my imagination, Captain, or is there smoke coming from inside the freighter?"

"Fire Vessel Anacortes back," another voice answered. "We've been watching that closely. There was concern about the possibility of fire. We're pretty certain there's a container or two with pyrotechnics still aboard. If they were somehow to be next to a source of heat...well, it's all hypothetical but...enough said."

The binoculars were making it too difficult to get a full picture of the scene, so Meagan lowered hers and shielded her eyes against the sun. She heard loud rumbling noises coming from the freighter. It sounded to her like the ship was moaning in agony.

"I think I can see it moving," she shouted.

"I'm pretty sure you're right," Kirby said from his post. He had a relieved look on his face. "Looks like we're going to have success today. Let's just hope nothing goes wrong as she comes off. I've heard they have several very large bilge pumps on board in case she takes on too much seawater as she comes off. They couldn't assess her bottom as thoroughly as they'd have liked since there were still containers near the hull breach obstructing their view."

The dying beast, *Bel Amica*'s groaning continued.

"There's more smoke," Meagan noted, thinking about those fireworks Kirby had mentioned. Meagan remembered fireworks left a characteristic-smelling smoke in their wake, smoke you could taste on the air on a Fourth of July evening. Perhaps the same smell she was experiencing now.

Kirby shrugged. "Like I said, those fireboats were probably brought here for a purpose. Looks like the tugs are letting up a little. She's probably off, or nearly so. Until they get that vessel to a dry dock, I wouldn't count on anything."

"Dry dock?" Meagan asked.

"That's a big, strong place where you can get the boat totally out of the water so you can work on her bottom."

"Work on her bottom? That's funny—you mean work on her bum."

Kirby smiled, as she lightened the mood.

The smoke she'd seen billowing up from the hull was getting thicker, a solid white against the darker *Bel Amica* mass.

Now it seemed to Meagan that the smell was not only that of fireworks. It smelled more electrical, like that time the car's wiring had overheated or when her dad's laptop had almost caught on fire.

"Those tugs will really have their work cut out getting her to the dry docks in Vancouver against the big ebb coming up," Kirby noted, "especially with all the swirling currents here in Haro. They'll be lucky just to keep her heading in the right direction with that rudder stuck all the way over, let alone making much headway. They've got about forty miles to go, so I'd guess it will take a day or so to get there."

One of the fireboats pulled up alongside the *Bel Amica*. Meagan watched as it began spraying something from its nozzle, something too white to be water.

"Foam," Kirby answered her unspoken question. "They must have real concerns about what's causing the smoke and that rumbling sound."

Meagan jumped as a muffled explosion carried across on the wind. It sounded like a gunshot. Then, like a machine gun firing in rapid succession, followed by more loud booms.

She looked up to Kirby to check his reaction. A dark expression crossed his face. He said, "That's not good."

Over the CB radio, they heard the fire boat captain shout, "More foam over there!"

More and more explosions could be heard coming from inside the freighter.

Kirby began to worry about whether they still had this under control. He tried to reassure Meagan that as long as they maintained hull integrity, everything should be fine. But still, he thought to himself, they may not have an unlimited supply of the fire retardant. Certainly not enough if a fireworks chain reaction happened.

Kirby's VHF came on. It was the Coast Guard calling the fireboat. "Captain Hunt."

"I read. Listen, I'm damned busy—"

"Captain Hunt, you may want to increase the retardant," the Coast Guard woman interrupted with the utmost diplomacy.

Hunt snorted, indicating he didn't have time for diplomacy. "I'm doing everything I can to keep these fireworks from blowing the place to Kingdom Come."

"Fireworks aren't the only volatile thing onboard." A pause. "The captain of the ship reported he thought he remembered seeing lithium ion batteries on the computer manifesto."

"Batteries?" Hunt repeated. "Like the Boeing Dreamliner battery problems that created extreme heat and even explosions? Oh god! *Now* you tell me!"

Chapter 17

"Shall I turn on the TV, Mr. Strander?" the nurse asked as she reached across Howard's bed for the remote control. As she fussed with his pillows and gathered up the remnants of his meal, the television flickered to life, the robotic voices of some local news station coming through.

"—heard some strange rumbling noise coming from the vessel a moment ago," the TV broadcaster said.

A second later the picture cleared, and Howard blinked at the familiarity of it. It was surreal to watch news coverage of the freighter on TV, especially when he had been right there not long ago. From the vantage point of the news helicopter high above the crystal-clear waters of the Salish Sea, he could see the shoulder of the rocky reef leading up to the pinnacle that had done the deed. The setting couldn't have been more picturesque, with the iconic red and white lighthouse built in 1936 setting the backdrop only a short distance away. With the gigantic freighter up on the rocks and dozens of smaller boats circling it, the entire scene looked like a pack of predators circling dying prey. Long columns of smoke billowed upwards towards the news copter. He wondered if the thick smoke was causing the coughing of the news crew.

A woman dressed in a smart suit appeared in front of the camera overlooking Turn Point, covering her mouth as she tried to talk. "Tom, we're getting reports that the Coast Guard is pushing back the safety zone."

The camera made another pan of the scene below. Looking closer, Howard could see the firefighters aboard the bright red ships as they hurried back and forth. The camera panned to the lighthouse area and he could see the shapes of people standing above it along the bluff, watching.

What's wrong with you? Howard screamed inside his head. *Can't you see the smoke? Get out of there!* His arms twitched, like when he watched a horror movie and saw the monster a split second before the character on screen did. *Is this another case where I'm letting my family down? Not being present...up to the task when really needed most?*

"Are you in any danger there, Michele?" an anchorman back in the studio asked, voicing Howard's concern.

"No," the reporter answered. "It appears authorities have it under control for the moment. We're being asked—"

It was difficult to tell what happened first: the explosion or the reeling of the camera. The entire shot went out of focus, and then more than one person was screaming.

Howard sat up straight; the nurse at his side jumped at the noise on the television. Together they watched as the cameraman regained control, righting the picture as best he could, though he was clearly shaken by whatever had just happened.

"Oh my God," the reporter's voice said breathlessly.

"Michele?" The anchorman's voice had an edge of hysteria to it. "Michele, what happened? Are you all right?"

"Tom, th-the freighter. That huge blast....it looks like the port side of the ship—right about where the pinnacle was—blew out...it's gone."

There was a shrieking noise in the background, followed by an explosion. And then another. It almost sounded like...yes, it was fireworks, because when the camera panned out to the sky, Howard could see the flashes of light and color even in broad daylight.

"W-we're fine," the reporter continued. "It looks like we're high enough to be out of range, but there are...uh, pyrotechnics going off in all directions." A blast of red and green lit up the side of her face, but she was gesturing towards the water again. "The explosions are dying down, now, but the ship...oh my God, it's going, Tom! It's going!"

It took a few seconds for the cameraman to steady the picture, but when he did, he caught the *Bel Amica* as it began to lean. Howard gripped the railing of his bed as he watched. Like a big goldfish gone belly-up, the boat rolled over, launching a wave at the nearby tugs and fireboats. They bobbed like rubber ducks in a tub.

"That was amazing," the reporter said as the wave dissipated.

The ship was completely submerged, a giant shadow lurking beneath the water's surface. A second or two passed in which the news crew tried to gather their collective breaths, and then the water started roiling.

"Michele," the anchorman back at the station said, "what's happening over there?"

"It's...something's trying to surface."

The camera zoomed in on where the bubbles churned the water near a fireboat. Something emerged from the depths and bobbed alongside the vessel.

"What is that?"

"It looks...it looks like a shipping container, Tom. Look, there's another one!"

The camera panned to show another container farther away making its way up. Then another, even farther away.

"We're getting news now," the reporter said, "that the Coast Guard is ordering all boats to leave the area. More containers are coming up as the ship is apparently rolling down an underwater bank." The containers continued to pop up farther and farther offshore. At least a couple dozen floating already. "They're saying the trench is five hundred feet deep here and there's a real danger to nearby craft. Just imagine what that could do to a boat bottom coming up from that deep."

At his side, Howard heard the nurse draw in a sharp gasp. No doubt she knew people who were at the scene right now. That was when the horrible thought surfaced: His family was out there! *And I'm just lying here helpless...while they're in harm's way!*

An hour earlier

After tying the jet ski to the Prevost State Park dock and ascending the ramp to the lighthouse trail, Jason's hand itched to take Sidney's hand, pull her aside, and tell her how much fun these last few days had been. Fun, but also terrifying. He wanted to tell her how amazing she was and thank her for helping save his father. The secluded, wooded paths up the Turn Point Trail seemed like the proper place to tell her all of this, except, well...apparently they weren't the only ones who'd had the idea to watch the ungrounding from the bluff.

He sighed in annoyance as a middle-aged, out-of-shape guy huffed along beside them, snapping pictures as he went. No matter how hard he tried to slow his steps, the guy would not take a hint and go ahead of them to join the rest of the gawkers. Sidney kept shooting Jason sympathetic glances, as if to say, "Can you believe this guy?" And walking faster wouldn't do any good because it would only put him and Sidney in the middle of the other group, who looked, from their T-shirts, like a Sea Scout troop coming over from their boat in Prevost to also witness the ungrounding.

Bordering the trail were wind-gnarled, old-growth Douglas firs that rose like pillars from the ground, the first branches a full story above the forest floor. Fallen branches here and there, fuzzy with moss, and prehistoric ferns snaked upwards towards an elusive sun.

Up ahead, the trees parted, revealing the bluff overlooking the ungrounding. Finally, *finally*, the guy with the camera jogged ahead to get a good spot for watching...only to turn back and catch a quick picture of the two of them. Jason lifted his hand against the man's camera's sightline.

"Ah, sorry about that," the man said, lowering the camera. "I was trying to get a picture of the trees. The two of you make a great couple, though. Say, do I know you two?" He held up his hand and snapped his fingers. "Yeah. Aren't you the two on the jet ski? You helped save that guy who fell in?" He snapped his fingers again. "Yeah, yeah. I saw you on TV last night."

"You did?"

"Yeah, on Cooper Andrews's segment. That was you, wasn't it?"

"Yes, sir," Sidney answered. "We had a hand in all that."

The man smiled and held out his hand. "Frank Litz, reality TV producer." He had a surprisingly firm handshake, though it was quick and perfunctory, as if he did this often with people whose names he never remembered. "I'm scouting out a location for our new show." He stepped back and held out his hands, as if dictating what should go on a marquee. "'Wet and Wild.' Like the name? I thought of it myself. It's a reality show where contestants face off in marine-based challenges. A little bit of survival, a little bit of competition, a little bit of teenaged drama. Fun for the whole family on Thursday nights, huh?"

Jason wondered if this guy just liked hearing himself talk or if there was a purpose to this.

"Are you both under eighteen? Because you two are made for TV. You ever done any acting? I'm looking for a couple who might get together on the show. Two young people from different backgrounds who find each other, that sort of thing. All very tasteful, of course. The folks will love it. Do you think you might be interested—if, of course, your parents approve?"

He talked so fast, Jason could hardly keep up with what he was saying.

Sidney seemed to be having just as much difficulty, because her brow became more wrinkled the more he talked. Finally, she held up a hand to stop him. "Uh, Mr. Litz…"

"Frank. Call me Frank. Oh, my card." He reached into the pocket of his Hawaiian shirt and pulled out two business cards. "You don't have to answer now. Just think about it, okay?" He gave them both a wink. "Casting call starts next month. You two should definitely—"

Jason felt the skin tingling on the back of his neck a split second before Sidney tensed at his side.

"Did you hear that?" she asked.

The three of them turned to the bluff. There was some kind commotion out there. Fireworks? The, eleven- and twelve-year-old Sea Scouts hopped up and down nervously as the two scout leaders tried to shepherd them away from the ledge.

The nice, peaceful walk along the trail was forgotten as Jason and Sidney hurried over. "What's going on?" Jason asked, craning his neck to see. Clouds of smoke filled the air, wafting upwards and towards them. They could already smell it from here. "It sounded like—"

An earth-shattering blast reached them and nearly knocked them off their feet. A wave of heat and smoke washed over the bluff, covering everything in a smoky haze. Their ears were ringing as they tried to get their bearings. Sound came back gradually, a chorus of screaming voices from inside the fog.

"Sidney?" Jason called and looked around for her.

"I'm here."

The smoke, smelling of fireworks, dissipated quickly on the wind.

"What was that!? An explosion of some kind. I thought it was an earthquake at first, but..." She trailed off as her gaze swept over the bluff and back up the trail. Jason saw her eyes go wide. This was the girl who did death-defying tricks on her jet ski. He wasn't sure he wanted to know what was capable of scaring her, but he also had a feeling he was about to find out.

His eyes followed her line of sight back to the top of the trail. Just over her shoulder, he could see another plume of smoke rising over the tree line. It smelled different than the smoke from the explosion, less like fireworks and more like a campfire. Gritty and earthy. He wondered what that meant.

"Fire," Sidney said. "It's so dry up here this time of year, I'll bet the explosion caught some brush on fire."

"We came from the fire's direction," Jason said. "Will we be able to get back to the dock?"

The scout leaders seemed to think so, because they were leading their scouts in that direction.

Sidney lifted her head. "Not good. Wind's heading southeast."

"What does that mean?"

"It means the fire is going to spread. And it'll be heading this way and toward the trail back to Prevost." She grabbed hold of his hand. "We need to get off this bluff. If we can make it to the shoreline, the Coast Guard might be able to get a boat in to get us out, but if we try to leave the way we came in..." Her wide-eyed stare was all the information he needed.

"Wait!" he screamed, running after the kids.

One of the two scout leaders turned in alarm to see him coming over the trail towards them. The leader tensed as Jason drew nearer, like he was some crazy person. He didn't really care at that moment.

"You can't go that way," he explained. "There's a fire. You're heading right toward it. Your trail will be cut off. You could get trapped heading back that way."

The woman leader grasped the pendant on her necklace and held it tight. "A fire?"

"We'll have to go around." Jason made a vague gesture back towards the bluff. "We can get a boat to lift us out of here."

"I don't know." The woman twirled her pendant between her fingers. "That sounds dangerous."

"You don't have a choice. If you keep going that way, you'll run right into the fire."

Her face paled at that. She turned around, cupped her hands to her mouth, and fairly shrieked, "Children! Children, get back here!"

The children came running back, as well as the other scout master. Mr. Litz came up to join their little huddle, and together Jason and Sidney detailed their escape plan.

"The best route is to follow the bluff until the cliff is less steep and we can get down to the shore," Sidney said. "We should get going now, though. There's no telling how fast that fire might move."

Mr. Litz raised his hand, as if he needed permission to ask a question. "I don't know if I could make it down that incline," he said, pointing. Sweat poured off his face and soaked his shirt. "Maybe we should try for the lighthouse? The fire couldn't reach us there, could it?"

Sidney considered it with a dubious look on her face. "It's mostly stone, so it probably wouldn't burn… Listen…we'll help you. You can do this."

"We'll stick together," Jason cut in. "Nobody gets left behind."

Sidney gave him an appreciative glance and nodded. "Okay, you heard him, people." She broke their circle as she began to walk quickly back towards the bluff, clapping her hands to spur them on. "I'll take the lead and, Jason, you take up the rear. We'll go as fast as we can safely. Anyone, call out if you have a problem. We're off!"

Chapter 18

M eagan tugged on Kirby's shirtsleeve. "Jason's up there."
It took the barest of moments for the meaning to sink in. His cell rang.
"Kirby, this is Jason."

"Jason, where are you? Meagan and I just saw those flames. Are you in trouble?"

"Yeah, we are. We're trying to outrun the fire by heading down the south shore bluff. A Sea Scout group and an old guy are with us. When we get to where we can climb down to the beach, just this way from those houses, can you meet us?"

"You bet. I'm headed your way. Wait…I need to talk to the Coast Guard first. But don't worry. I won't leave you stranded. I'll be there." Kirby immediately reached for his radio. "Coast Guard," he barked. "This is Kirby Jackson."

"Copy," a harried voice came back. "Coast Guard cutter Warren Magnuson here. We're a little overbooked right now, so we're keeping this line open for emergencies only."

"Sir?" Kirby would have laughed if the situation had allowed it. "You know me…from the Whale Research Center. What's the situation with the brush fire?"

The coast guardsman sighed. "We have a couple planeloads of fire retardant coming in, but God only knows when they can get here. Certainly that's the only way we have a chance to save those homes a mile or so down the beach."

"Look, I don't know if you folks are aware, but there were people on the bluff watching the ungrouding. Now the fire is pushing them down those bluffs on the south shore."

"That's not good. I'll see if there's a boat we can divert that way."

"Actually, I think I can get there faster. I'm out on the water here, near the safety zone. It's about, let's see…two miles from here. I can be there in less than five minutes."

"Negative, can't have civilians endangering themselves or others —"

"Noted," Kirby said, "but I'm not exactly a typical civilian and I'm closer than you. By the time you get someone in there, all those hikers could be…" He turned to see Meagan's eyes grow wide. "In serious jeopardy," he finished.

The guardsman sighed again. "If *we* have to bail *you* out…"

"You won't." Kirby pushed the forward throttle on the pontoon. "We've got this."

Jason turned to look behind. The fire was definitely headed their way now and closing fast. Amidst the gray plumes of smoke, tongues of orange and red flickered hungrily at the dry brush. He could feel the heat carried on the updraft, sweat already plastering his shirt to his back. He hollered for the group to pick up the pace.

They'd gone about a mile, heading downslope and downwind, Sidney in the lead and Jason bringing up the rear. Some of the Sea Scouts were having difficulty keeping up, and he was there to get them moving if they slowed or stopped for too long. It was actually the TV producer, Mr. Litz, who was giving him the most trouble, though. The man was clearly out of shape, and he had to stop every hundred paces or so to bend over and catch his breath. His face was a brilliant red and dripping with sweat. He'd come here looking to set up the filming of a reality TV show, but this was probably more reality than he'd bargained for.

The downward tilt of the bluff to the water was steep, with loose rocks at the precipice of deep gullies. Sidney was up front helping the kids and their chaperones to keep from slipping. The kids managed it better than Litz or the chaperones.

"They're always making us do fire drills at school," one of the boys had muttered to Jason. "*They're* the ones who are always saying you need to keep calm in emergencies."

Jason agreed, though it was becoming more and more difficult to maintain his patience when Mr. Litz slipped, again, and nearly tumbled head over heels down over the bluff. Jason reached out and yanked him back to his feet just in time, and Mr. Litz gave him a grateful smile. His smile quickly gave way, though, as Jason tried to urge him forward. One step and his face contorted in pain.

"I think I sprained it," he said, bending down to rub at his ankle.

Jason was at his side, steadying him. "Can you walk?"

"I don't know. I...maybe?" He took another step and his foot went out from under him. His arms flailed and he reached out for Jason, nearly taking them both down. Litz slipped and slid down a gully, until he came to an abrupt halt against a rock.

"Mr. Litz!" Jason hurried down to help him, mindful of the crumbly rocks giving way under his feet. "Mr. Litz, are you okay?"

"I'm...okay, but I don't think I can go on."

Sidney had stopped to see what the holdup was.

Jason waved her off. "Get the scouts to the shore. I'll help Mr. Litz."

She looked like she wanted to protest but simply nodded. She cupped her hands and called up the ridge, "I'll be back. Just hold on, okay?" And then she was following the Sea Scouts down towards the rocky shore to get them to the water where the flames couldn't get them.

Moments later, Jason looked to the west over his shoulder at the sound of a plane coming in low. Directly up the slope from them, it released its red shower of retardant onto the leading edge of the windblown flames.

The flames were getting closer and hotter with each passing moment, but it was the smoke that choked the air and made it difficult to breathe. Jason pulled his shirt up over his mouth, a sort of makeshift air filter. It didn't do much, but it was better than nothing. When he looked back up the ridge, he could see a rogue tongue of the fire not affected by the retardant approaching him. Jason could see Sidney and her cadre a few hundred yards ahead. She and the scout troop had waded out onto one of the larger rocks, the waves from passing boats breaking roughly over it and soaking everyone up to the knees.

They were waving their arms, and he followed their gazes out along the water until he saw what they had seen: a bright orange craft coming straight for them.

He knew that craft. Kirby!

It was hard going, the waves choppy from all the big cruisers heading back down the channel from the sinking, but Kirby wasn't about to let that slow him down. An eighty-foot monster yacht passed going fifteen knots and throwing a four-foot wake. It looked to Kirby as if his relatively miniscule craft was facing the perfect storm. He pulled back all the way on the throttle, slowing his pontoon boat, but still went airborne as they were hit by the gigantic wave.

He bent his knees as the boat crashed down, clacking his teeth together. He saw Meagan stumble and grab the side of the boat, her small but strong hands finding a rope handle. "You okay?" he called. She turned back and nodded, a determined look on her face. Kirby nodded back and quickly got up to full throttle, taking the smaller two-foot, jaw-rattling waves head on.

"I see them!" Meagan cried as she pointed towards the shore.

Kirby could see them too, a little group silhouetted against the grayish black rocks just ahead. Over a dozen arms waved in the air, drawing him in with their frantic movements. The fire looked to be within a couple hundred feet and swooping down toward them. As he approached, a few embers fell onto his boat and he could feel the heat of the fire.

Kirby slowed as he neared the shoreline, looking out for barely submerged rocks. The last thing he needed was a broken prop during a rescue mission. Seeing no obstacles, he nosed the bow right up against the rock, where the group was standing. One of the adults cried, "Thank heavens," as the other adult began pushing the children over the gunnel one at a time.

Sidney gripped the side of the boat to keep it anchored as Kirby grabbed the scouts' arms to assist them in climbing aboard. The boat wasn't Coast Guard approved for this many people, but they were small and Kirby could make do if they packed in like sardines, regardless of regulations. Sidney interrupted his thoughts. "Jason's still up on the bluff." Kirby could hear pain in her voice. "The old guy hurt himself trying to get down, so Jason stayed behind to help him," she said.

Kirby looked up at the spreading fire. Bits of ember and ash were raining down on them now. He could see why she was worried. Then another plane approached, this one coming from the east. Kirby expected more retardant, but to his surprise, parachutes unfurled above the narrowing space between the fire and houses.

"Jason's not too far up the slope," Sidney shouted. "If you have a rope…"

"Do I have a rope?" Kirby smirked. "Who do you think you're talking to, young lady? Of course I have a rope."

She gave him an uncertain grin. "If I can get that rope up to Jason, we could use it to lower Mr. Litz down from the bluff."

"Sounds like a plan."

The last of the children had gotten on, followed by the two adult chaperones. Sidney pushed the boat back, freeing it of the rocks, and jumped on the bow. Some of the children and even one of the adults cheered, but Sidney didn't look like she was too interested in their accolades.

"Here you go." Kirby reached under his steering console and found a braided nylon tow rope he hoped would work. He tossed it to her, and she caught it. Gripping it tightly, she made her way back to the bow and perched there. "Hold on. We're on our way."

⸙

Jason watched as the bright orange craft pulled away from the rocks, did a quick turnabout, and came in close to where he was doing his level best to keep Mr. Litz from freaking out. Jason was relieved to see Sidney standing at the bow, a length of rope of her hands. As they neared the shore, she tossed

it, sending it flying end over end, as high up the rocky slope as she could. She wasn't far behind, making a leap onto a large boulder just below where the rope had landed. She picked up the rope and climbed to where she threw a few loops to Jason's feet. He gripped it and began making a little loop at one end before kneeling down at Mr. Litz's side.

"Mr. Litz…Frank," he began in a slow, calm way, "I'm going to lasso your upper torso with the rope, okay?" To demonstrate, he pushed a large loop of rope through the smaller loop. He lifted it over Litz's head and shoulders and tightened it under his armpits. "I'm going to place a couple of loops around that tree above us here." He pointed to a sturdy-looking juniper tree and hoped it would hold Mr. Litz's weight. "As I feed out rope, we're going to lower you down the embankment slowly. Understand?"

Mr. Litz nodded.

"Good. If you feel yourself getting hung up, don't worry because I've got the other end of the rope around your legs, so Sidney will be in position to pull you away from the rocks.

Your weight should do most of the work." Now was not the appropriate time, but he hoped the older man didn't take that the wrong way. "You got it?"

Mr. Litz shifted himself and grunted painfully. "I think so. My ankle really hurts. I'll do my best, though."

Jason helped him stand and, allowing Mr. Litz to lean heavily on him, they made their way to the steeply sloping ledge. Jason placed two loops around the juniper, yanked on it a few times to test its strength, then gave Mr. Litz a thumbs up sign. With a nervous gulp, Mr. Litz began to lower himself down the side of the steep bluff.

Twice, he wasn't able to push off to maintain his descent and Sidney had to reach up to jerk on his feet to free him from where he was wedged in rocky crevasses.

When he got to the bottom, Kirby moved the boat in closer. He barked at the two scout masters to help, and each took an arm and began hauling him aboard. Sidney, who had retreated back down to a partially submerged rock next to the bow, took hold of his legs and helped lift his dead-weight torso over the bow. The entire boat tilted at the added weight.

Jason watched nervously from above. He saw the wave coming before Kirby did. Just as they had gotten Mr. Litz to counterbalance, the swell of the giant wave lifted the boat from behind. "Watch out!" Jason cried, and by some miracle, Kirby was able to throw the boat into reverse quick enough to keep the bow from slamming Sidney into the rock wall behind her.

Instead, she was washed off the rock by the tall breaker as it hit her. She went under and disappeared from sight.

"Sidney!" Jason shouted.

Before he could do something stupid, like throw himself in after her, she bobbed to the surface a safe distance from shore. Her hat was gone, and her hair clung in limp knots around her face. Her voice was a bit hoarse when she shouted, "Darn, wish I could have caught that one on my jet ski."

Jason let out a sigh of relief.

"Jason, hurry up!" Kirby shouted.

He did not need to be told twice. Forgoing the rope altogether, he began climbing down the rock face, searching with his fingers and toes for grips. By the time he reached the bottom, Sidney had climbed back onboard. "Jump," she called. He let go of the rock and jumped the last three feet onto the pontoon boat's gunnel, bouncing and rolling on the waves.

The Sea Scouts cheered, and Mr. Litz began clapping. Even the scout masters and Kirby joined in.

Sidney ran up and threw her arms around Jason's neck. Her skin was cold and wet, but Jason hugged back. "Don't scare me like that again," she said.

"Same goes for you."

"Me? I just went for a little swim." She pulled back and began wringing the water from her hair. "You should have joined me. It really feels good after being so close to that hot fire."

"Maybe later," he laughed as he turned to Kirby. "Can we get back to terra firma, preferably someplace that's not on fire?"

"Right-o." Kirby hurriedly turned the boat one hundred eighty degrees and headed back toward Roche Harbor.

Looking from Kirby's vessel toward the homes in jeopardy, they watched a virtual army fighting the fire with apparent progress. People were wetting down their roofs with garden hoses. An ancient bulldozer was carving a brush-free firebreak in front of the homes, and paratroopers were doing hand work near the dozer. One of the fireboats had gotten as close as it could and seemed to be reaching the two homes closest to the beach with a welcome shower.

Looking to the west, Sidney shouted, "Look, another plane."

"Probably more retardant, to seal the deal," Kirby said. "Might be interesting to continue watching, but I'm focused on getting all of you back to safety so your parents can relax."

Chapter 19

"Three cheers for the rescuers, our heroes. Hip, hip..."

"Hurray!" The bar patrons joined in, lifting their drinks to toast with the nearest person.

"Yes, cheers for the adventurers," Karen muttered, "but they better not do it ever again." She turned and swatted her son on the shoulder. "You scared me to death."

Jason wasn't sure how many times he was going to have to apologize to his mother. She'd seen the entire thing, watching it on TV at the hospital. In fact, they'd barely gotten to the dock in Roche Harbor before Karen, Tanya, and Doug were all there, clamoring to see their children. Hugs had been shared, grateful kisses exchanged. The EMTs asked if any of Kirby's passengers needed medical attention. No one had been seriously hurt, but Mr. Litz was taken away on a stretcher to a waiting van for transport to the hospital to treat his badly swollen ankle.

Doug announced, "Drinks on me. I'm taking everybody to the bar to celebrate our heros being alive."

Jason, Sidney, and Meagan sat at a table on the deck just outside the open bar door and sipped their sodas. Even heroes weren't allowed inside if they weren't twenty-one. Jason stirred his drink with his flimsy straw and watched the others. Meagan was retelling the tale, complete with expressive hand movements, and every so often Kirby would join in with gestures of his own. Karen looked quietly reflective as the stories went on, but Doug just laughed and Tanya continued to hug her daughter.

Jason was exhausted beyond words and content to sit and watch, through the open bar door, at the news unfolding on the TV screen mounted above the intricately carved turn-of-the-century oak bar.

"The Coast Guard is ordering every boat out of Boundary Pass two miles north and south of Turn Point," a male anchor reported over footage of the watery scene below. "Boats in Prevost and Reid Harbors are to exit to the east past Johns Island."

Several Coast Guard vessels appeared on the screen, along with shots of the occasional new container shooting to the surface, with the dozens already there and beginning to drift with the ebb tide current to the south.

The television reporter stated, "The U.S. and Canadian Coast Guards are reported to have called for more tugs to corral the floating containers."

Jason shrugged. He was exhausted from the heat and all the day's activities and about ready to fall asleep in his own lemonade.

Kirby seemed to notice and gave him a rough pat on the back. Turning to Karen, he said, "I think your kids have had enough for one day. Why don't you take them back to their rooms to get some rest?"

Karen was only too willing to oblige. She ushered Meagan and Jason away, but when she tried to pay the tab, three different patrons jumped in to offer their money. In the end, the bartender told them drinks were on him.

"Thank you," Karen said. "You've all been so kind."

The bartender waved her off. "You're local heroes, likely to go down in island lore for keeping the orcas and Mosquito Pass oil free, after all this mess is over."

Just as they were about to leave the bar, the helicopter reporter's voice excitedly exclaimed, "Well, folks, it's been quite a day. I don't recall another quite like it in my career. For the record, the fire looks to be under control. You can see some residual smoke from smoldering brush, but no flames. With the tinder so dry, I expect the fire folk will keep working and will keep a keen eye out for flare-ups. No new containers have come up from the depths for the last ten minutes, but the Coast Guard is likely to prohibit any boat traffic anywhere near here until they're certain the last ones have come up. I assume traffic will be routed well to the west somewhere near the U.S.-Canadian boundary. So that will do it from here, and we'll send it back to station headquarters."

Getting up from his bar stool, Kirby announced, "See you all at the concert tomorrow. Should be interesting, as we have lots to reflect on and much to celebrate. Knowing Vern Olsen and the Shifty Sailors as I do, I don't doubt they'll capture the significance of the week's events appropriately." Raising his glass to everyone one more time, he walked toward the door.

Jason was about ready to keel over, but Meagan was still a ball of energy. She bounced to Kirby's side and announced, "When I get older, I'm going to work for you so I can help the orcas and people like you."

"I don't doubt for one minute that you will," Kirby laughed. "We need young folks like you to come along and replace the old codgers like me. I can't do this forever."

———— ∞∞ ————

Jason was looking forward to sleeping in a real bed again, but as Karen and the Andersons waited in the hotel lobby for the elevator doors to open, Sidney quietly grabbed his hand and led him outside. They rounded a corner into a narrow secluded space between two of the restored historic buildings, one an old ice shed.

He felt his heart kick into overdrive. "What's up, Sid?"

She smiled coyly at him. "We might not get many more chances to be alone."

He smiled. "I'm afraid you're right. In a day or two, when Dad's ready, we'll leave for home. I'm...I'm really going to miss you."

"I feel the same way," Sidney said. "I've sure had fun."

"We can text."

She nodded.

Jason took a deep breath. "Sid, would you mind a goodbye kiss?"

She said nothing, but reached up and pulled his head down. As they moved apart a little, Sidney said, "Every time we use the word 'ice,' it can refer to a kiss. So, like, if I say the weather's fine, but it's a little 'icy,' we can pretend. Or if it's hot out and I text I really need an 'iced mocha,' you'll know what I mean."

"It won't be the same," Jason said, "but I guess that's about as good as we can do from fifteen hundred miles apart." He laced their fingers together as they stood in their little hidden nook near the ice shed. "How about a little ice for a nightcap?"

Chapter 20

A fter things had quieted down from the day's extraordinary events, Karen caught a ride to the hospital. As Karen entered Howard's room, he looked away from the TV. He raised his arms in an embracing gesture, and began to whimper as they hugged. "Karen, I was so scared. Look what I caused. Jason could have..."

"Stop, honey. You haven't done anything wrong. Jason's fine. But I think I know how you feel. It was frightening to watch. I'm not saying I wasn't worried too, but look at the bright side. Nobody was seriously hurt. Jason and Sidney are seen as heroes. Heaven knows what would have happened to those scouts and that older fellow if Jason and Sidney hadn't stayed focused and gotten them to safety. Jason has certainly matured and Sidney had the adventure of her life through all this. Megan's learned the equivalent of a college course in marine biology with a specialty in cetaceans. Howard, honey, please look at the bigger picture. The orcas are untouched by oil, thanks in large part to you calling in quickly to Orca Network. Some of the most fragile shoreline is untouched. Again, you played a role. An old freighter is gone. But more than one person has assured you that you shouldn't attribute any fault to yourself. No homes were lost to the fire. And most important of all to me, you're going to be fine."

Karen hugged Howard tighter to emphasize her points.

After a prolonged embrace, Howard said, "I guess you're right. I just got so scared watching that fire on TV racing toward Jason and Sidney... I'm just so thankful... Maybe I'm suffering from a post-traumatic stress type thing."

"You'll be fine in time, honey. You just need some rest and for things to quiet down. God knows you've been through a lot. Tomorrow we should be back together again as a family. Do you want me to stay the night? The kids would be fine. The Andersons offered to watch out for them were I to stay here tonight."

"No, I'll be fine now. You've helped me feel much better. Now the kids might need you to help decompress."

Karen planted a long, sweet kiss on Howard's lips then rushed off to catch the last shuttle van back to Roche Harbor.

The next afternoon on the lawn just up the hill from the Roche docks, the smoky sweet smell of barbeque wafted over the area. White tables with striped tablecloths bore all manner of food for concert-goers. The local maritime fare of salmon and prawns was generously augmented with hamburgers, hotdogs, ribs, and chicken. Salads of all sorts—potato, pasta, green, and fruit—had been set out to be picked over. Desserts were dominated by Whidbey Pies' offerings of boysenberry, loganberry, and marionberry a la mode.

Everybody was in an almost giddy mood. It was a bright, warm summer day, not a cloud in the sky, perfect for a celebratory event. Meagan, Jason, and Sidney mingled with the slightly older youth volunteers who predominated.

Howard, newly back from the hospital but still in a wheelchair, was pushed along by Karen. Whenever someone called out to ask how he was doing, Howard was flabbergasted that anyone wanted to thank him for everything he'd done or even recognized him.

A loud screech from the speakers had everyone turning towards the stage, where Vern Olsen of the Shifty Sailors was fine-tuning the microphone. Dressed in the same blue and white striped sailor shirt he wore in Friday Harbor, mic in hand, he stepped forward to the anticipatory cheers of the crowd.

"Hey there, folks," he said while the rest of the Shifty Sailors tuned their instruments behind him. "We're all lucky to be gathered here today for this celebration. One hundred percent of any donations today will go to the ongoing clean-up efforts, and I know many of you here have already done more than your share to help out, whether you gave money or time. So let's give all our volunteer workers a big hand."

A round of applause swept through the concert area.

"I'd also like to take a second to extend an extra special thank you to a very special family." He put a hand to his eyes and scanned the crowd. "Stranders? Stranders, where are you? There you are." He waved to them. "Get on up here."

Karen blinked, but then Meagan and Jason were heading for the stage and she had no choice but to join them, pushing Howard as she went. Several stage-hands helped Karen lift Howard's wheelchair onto the stage, and Vern waited for the applause to die down again before continuing.

"These fine folks have been lending a hand literally since things started getting out of hand. So in honor of the Strander family, and especially Meagan's love of orcas, this song is dedicated to you."

They launched into the song they'd played at Friday Harbor, "Lolita, Come Home," now with new verses:

Meagan's desire was to observe orcas in the Salish Sea,
To enjoy seeing orcas living wild and free.
Meagan's enthusiasm swelled after a visit to the Whale Museum.
She could hardly wait to see em'.

Her sighting was delayed by an unseen event,
As she witnessed firsthand a freighter's bottom rent.
Its bunker fuel threatened to have the local waters oiled.
The Salish Sea and its inhabitants would likely both be spoiled.

But for the family's heroics and near-lethal efforts,
It could have spelled the end of her orca cohorts.
Without the work of SOSA and environmentalists,
The orcas and pristine environs would likely have ceased to exist.

As the song concluded with everybody joining in another round of the chorus, there was a standing ovation for the Shifty Sailors.

"Thank you for that, Vern," said Shannon, coming to the forefront with her own mic in hand with Jack by her side. It was strange to finally meet the people the Stranders had been speaking with over their cellphone and VHF radio for the past several days. The crowd cheered for them as well, so Howard surmised they must be popular local celebrities. "And thank you, Stranders. For all you've done."

"I'd just like to take a moment to say," Jack cut in, as Shannon handed the mic to him, "that some people, not knowing the area well and all the circumstances, might jump to the conclusion that the Stranders' sailboat caused the grounding. But let me tell you, nothing could be further from the truth. In my mind—and I *do* know the area and the circumstances very well—this type of incident was inevitable. These folks were victims of circumstances. If it hadn't been them, it would have been some other family under similar circumstances. But we're lucky it *was* them. Any other family might have slunk off and hid out of fear of retribution, but not the Stranders. No, they stuck around and did heroic work, as did many of you, to minimize the oil's effects."

"The fact is," Shannon said, as the two of them juggled the microphone between them, "that while this was indeed a significant environmental setback, it *could* have been so much worse. It could have been a laden tanker that went aground. It could have happened in the winter, with high wind and rough seas. I could go on and on. It's just incomprehensible."

"Could I say something?" Howard raised his hand weakly. Karen rolled him forward, and Jack tilted his head down and held the mic steady in front of him. As he began, his voice was thin and reedy, still not fully recovered from his ordeal. But as he went on, he gathered strength. At this point the crowd had swelled to several hundred. As Howard spoke, they became more and more silent until he had everyone's attention.

"I want to thank everyone for their kindness to me and my family. Over the last few days, lying in my hospital bed, I've been thinking about all the events and circumstances that have led up to the spill and this moment. I've even been analyzing the word 'spill.' I used to think of a spill as a freak thing that happened for no particular reason. I now think most things happen for a reason...making them somewhat predictable. Kids that are just learning to drink out of a glass... it's predictable they will spill their milk. Thinking about the oil spill, I now see it as somewhat predictable...not as to specific time, place, or circumstances... but its inevitability, predictable. As Kirby has explained, if you send enough ships up a narrow passageway with strong current in fog, with lots of other vessel in the vicinity, a grounding or collision will eventually happen. Mechanical systems fail. People err. Events in my own life illustrate the predictability principle. Karen and I need to talk a little more, but we agree we need to make some changes to prevent a spill in our family's life...and maybe we can move out here to help prevent a big spill in your Salish Sea. Seriously, why are we even considering taking on the increased risk of a major spill just to ship coal to China and tar sands oil to Asia? The warming of our environment caused by the burning of fossil fuels in just the last years has caused the most powerful storms ever in super-typhoon Haiyan and super-storm Sandy, while unprecedented tornados have ravaged the Great Plains and the west burns. Different parts of the world have seen record droughts, mudslides, fires, and floods. What's it going to take to wake us up? Hopefully our decision to move out here can help in some small way. My throat is getting very sore so I can't say more now. Again, thank you all very much."

The crowd jumped to its feet and wildly cheered for what seemed like forever.

Vern took the mic and appealed to the crowd, "Give me just a few seconds." He appeared to close his eyes in deep thought.

Everybody wondered what he was up to. After a few moments, he announced he'd thought up a new verse to his song. He grabbed his accordion and launched into it. The other Shifty Sailors picked up the melody.

The Stranders are going home to pack.
So they can make good on their commitment to come back.
They'll then be able to work to foil
The effort to bring more tankers laden with oil.

Vern shouted to the crowd, "Join us in the chorus."

Come home, Lolita! Lolita, come home!
You can swim in Puget Sound. This place is still your home.
Your pod is here to help you, to help you freely roam.
Come home, Lolita! Lolita, come back to an oil-free home!

———— ∞∞∞ ————

The next morning, after luxuriating in a gratis brunch buffet enjoyed by the Strander and Anderson families, Karen flicked the clasps on her suitcase. "Ready to go, hon?"

Howard was still rummaging around in the hotel bathroom. As she came around the corner, she saw him leaning against the counter, a bottle of pills in his hands. He was studying the label intensely. "These are the pills Dr. Singh gave me for the pain," he said, almost to himself.

"OxyContin?" she asked.

He examined the prescription bottle for a few more seconds before setting it resolutely back on the counter. "Ask the hotel if they have a place to dispose of prescription medications. My pain is gone. I won't need these anymore."

Karen wrapped her arms around his neck and, looking intently into Howard's eyes, kissed him passionately.

Both Jason and Meagan had disappeared, so Karen called the bellboy to help get their luggage down to the waiting van. She left Howard in his wheelchair by the front lobby and headed down to the marina in search of Meagan and Jason.

The fair weather had held, and the marina was alive with different types and sizes of boats with colorful yacht club pennants and flags. Karen took in the scene of vessels stretching all the way across Roche Harbor Marina and Mosquito Pass to Henry Island. As she looked to the southwest, much to her surprise, she saw the *Serendipity* swing around the point leading into the marina, with none other than Jason at the controls. Sidney followed behind in her jet ski.

She waved them over to the guest dock and helped Jason land the *Serendipity*.

"Well, look at you," she said, "aren't you becoming quite the sailor? This is a surprise. I didn't know you were planning to bring the *Serendipity* here."

"Mom," Jason said, waving off her teasing. "I just wasn't comfortable leaving it there unattended. The outboard motor looked like it was an easy target for the wrong kind of person. I just thought it was better to bring it here for the charter company's pick-up. Besides, we had a good tide in our favor, so it was easy and we weren't gone that long."

Karen laughed at his defensiveness. "Probably a good decision," she admitted. "Besides, we still have a few little things I'd like to get off the boat." She put her hands on her hips and looked around the docks. "Have you seen your sister anywhere?"

"I saw her with Kirby."

As if on cue, a now-familiar inflatable orange craft came skimming along the calm water. Kirby waved to them as he pulled up alongside the dock to let Meagan out.

"Mom, Kirby was just showing me that the speakers we put in the water definitely stopped the orcas from going straight into the oil. We saw them heading just north of Limekiln Point, following the salmon. Judging by the course they stayed on, I suspect they would have just followed the same course into the slick."

"That's great," Karen said. "It makes all we went through, particularly Dad, worthwhile. Of course, we were just bit players compared to you, Mr. Jackson."

"Now, now," Kirby wagged his finger at her. "My friends call me Kirby. And aside from the orcas, all of you are my new best friends."

The minute landing strip was only a stone's throw away, and their personal pilot for the morning still had the plane's engines running from his landing a few minutes earlier. He introduced himself as Mel. "So, the Orca Network asked me, as a board member, to personally fly you down to Anacortes as a token of our thanks for all you've done for the orcas," he said with a wide grin. "Would you like to take a little air tour, first? The islands look completely different from above."

"We have plenty of time," Howard answered. "Sounds great."

"I'm at your disposal," Mel said.

The plane was small and near capacity. Howard sat up front with Mel while Karen sat behind Mel, Jason behind Howard, with Meagan in the jump seat.

Mel checked everyone's seatbelt and informed them, "You're fortunate it's so clear out. You're going to see some beautiful country today."

The plane taxied down the runway, gaining speed. The whole carriage swayed as the wheels left the ground, and soon the earth was shrinking away from under them. The islands became masses of dark green against the aqua green water.

Mel pulled the mouthpiece down from his earphone and said through a speaker, "Shannon tells me K and L Pods were at Active Pass heading south a couple of hours ago, so keep your eye out for whale-watching boats. We might get lucky."

"That would be so cool!" Meagan said. "I'd love to see the other pods."

The plane flew over the Canadian border and Bedwell Harbor, at the south end of North Pender Island. Then it flew high over Active Pass—appropriately named, as it appeared narrow and busy with boat traffic and had visibly strong currents that coursed between two large islands Mel identified as Mayne and Galliano.

The whale-watching boats were out in full force. Squinting against the sun, the family could see the orcas' black shapes underwater and their telltale black fins cutting white streaks as they broke through the surface.

"Look, Mom," Meagan said excitedly. "There's one jumping—I mean breaching. K and L Pods are residents, just like J Pod, right? That means they stay mostly close by, doesn't it, sir?" she shouted over the engine noise, addressing Mel.

"So," Mel laughed into the speaker, "you're the aspiring young orca expert Shannon was talking about."

"I'm not an expert," Meagan responded, "but I sure do like them, and I think I might want to study and work with them some day."

"You're studying them right now and have been all week. The practical knowledge you've gained by being around the orcas, Kirby, and the Orca Network staff is invaluable when it comes to understanding orcas."

They turned and headed south over Saanich Inlet and were soon over Butchart Gardens, alive with color even from the air.

Mel commented, "Glad to see the oil doesn't appear to have come over the top of the peninsula and down to the gardens."

A few miles farther south and they were over Victoria and the famous Empress Hotel across the street from the Victoria marina, Mel pointing all the landmarks out in rapid-fire succession.

Heading east over Discovery and adjacent islands, Mel brought the plane to nearly the water level. He pointed out a thin band of oil clearly visible at the high tide line on one beach.

Progressing across Haro Strait toward the west side of San Juan Island, Dallas Mountain was visible ahead. Limekiln Point and Ralph Monroe Outlook appeared below. "Those are," Mel pointed out, "the most popular spots to watch for orcas from land."

They followed the San Juan Island coast southeast toward Salmon Banks and Eagle Point. Salmon seiners there were busy fishing sockeye salmon, their nets making the shape of a U. Mel explained that the orcas' echolocation allowed them to avoid the nets by going around or underneath, as opposed to the 1970 Penn Cove captures, where hunters had closed off the cove with nets that reached the bottom. He pointed out it was now illegal to capture orcas in Washington waters with any method.

Meagan interrupted, "But they still have Lolita."

"We're working on that, young lady," Mel quipped.

Mel identified Cattle Point, a national park, just ahead and San Juan Pass, separating San Juan and Lopez Islands. The south shore of Lopez Island was marked by indentations and a rugged coast, Mel explained, due to its being exposed to the Straits which connected unimpeded to the oftentimes misnamed Pacific Ocean.

Whale-watching boats lay ahead just off Iceberg Point. Some kayakers floated among the whales, exciting envy in Meagan.

"When we move here, can I get a kayak?"

"Maybe you can guide kayak whale-watching tours someday," Howard replied over his shoulder. "Who knows, it's all up to you?"

The small plane headed east across Rosario Straits towards Deception Pass. Deception Island lay just in front of the bridge and pass of the same name. Mel explained, "When Captain Vancouver was looking for the Northwest Passage, to save time getting to the Orient by not having to go around South America, he thought for a moment this might be the long sought after entrance. But it wasn't—hence 'deception.'

"The land to the south of the bridge is Whidbey Island." Mel explained he lived fifty miles to the south, on the southernmost end of the long, skinny island. A ferry connected the southern end to the mainland, but there was no south island bridge, which he explained suited the residents there just fine. They were fond of what Mel called their "rural character."

They swung back north, flying over East Sound and then Mt. Constitution on Orcas Island. Mt. Constitution was part of a state park, with views over the neighboring islands in all directions and back east to the mainland, Anacortes, and the Cascade Mountains. The white smoke belching from Anacortes's refinery just ahead was in stark contrast to the snowcapped Cascades in the background. One tanker unloaded while another waited at anchor.

"The oil comes from the north slope of Alaska, via Valdez and Prince William Sound," Mel said. "The tankers are now double-hulled, so they're a little less risky than before."

"Less risk," Howard said, leaning his head against the window. "But not *no* risk."

As they circled around again, Howard's gaze took in the beautiful blue and green of the San Juan Islands, pristine and unspoiled. It was odd to think that after everything he and his family had gone through, they'd still been lucky. Things could have been much, much worse.

No, he thought, making a silent vow to himself right then and there. *I'm going to make sure that big spill never happens. I'm going to do my part to protect this place.*

Then after a moment of reflection he announced, "We're moving. This is going to be our new home!"

Meagan shouted, "Yes"!

END

EPILOGUE

The March 24, 1989 Exxon Valdez oil spill devastated the people, environment and economy of Prince William Sound and far beyond. Fishermen and ancillary businesses suffered huge losses. Their boats, permits and way of life were destroyed. Spill workers suffered greatly, completely unaware of the toxicity of their work situation, and uninformed by Exxon about the health effects of aerosol polyaromatic hydrocarbons (PAHs) and beach cleaning solvents. Many died after years of debilitating illness. Exxon spent millions fighting attempts by the injured to prove correlation between their ailments and exposure.

The social effects were equally devastating. Post-traumatic stress, suicide, insomnia, divorce and depression were commonplace. Again Exxon fought all claims, repeatedly appealing any judgements until obtaining a ruling that gutted compensation to meaningless levels, and which came only after many claimants had died.

Hundreds of thousands of birds and marine mammals expired. Prince William Sound orcas lost much of their population at the time of the spill and have had poor calving since. The AT1 transient pod will all but certainly go extinct. Pre-spill there was a robust Prince William Sound herring biomass with an annual commercial harvest, but none since. Beaches, that appear on casual observation, to be oil free after almost three decades, reveal significant oil in the substrate upon turning over rocks or digging. Clams and many smaller creatures that form the base of the food web are unrecovered.

Exxon assured everybody of the safety of their enterprise, saying a large spill all but couldn't happen. But, if such an unimaginable event should occur, its clean up preparedness would take care of things in rapid order. Nothing could have been further from the truth. Immediately following the spill there was virtually no cleanup of any significance in spite of three day of calm weather. Some reputable scientists have even claimed the futile 'cleanup' effort did more harm than good. A recent study commissioned by the State of Washington found that only forty percent of a 200,000 gallon spill would be recovered in the first forty eight hours under 'ideal' circumstances. Imagine how little of a multimillion gallon spill would be recovered under, the usual, less than ideal circumstances.

Is it worth the risk for an oil company and its ancillary businesses to profit for a few years while the threat of an Exxon Valdez magnitude spill increases? If the Trans Mountain Pipeline is permitted bringing bituminous tar sand oil to Vancouver for trans-shipment down Boundary Pass and Haro Strait, the chances of a disaster will increase significantly. Tanker transport will go from five Exxon Valdez size tankers a month to thirty five and they will be transporting a near impossible to recover or clean up form of crude. If such an event were to occur in the Salish Sea, the economic, social and environmental cost to the area would be unimaginable.

The debacle in Prince William Sound is a clear warning of what could happen here with increased tanker traffic. Our area is known for fog, strong tides and a high volume of recreational boat traffic. Contrast this with clear, calm weather and no distracting boat traffic at the time of the Exxon spill. The world is awash in oil now. Breakthroughs in battery technology and sustainable energy are in the news. We must take advantage of and support these new developments and save our Salish Sea ecosystem.

30465686R00115

Made in the USA
Middletown, DE
26 March 2016